Praise for Mar *d Lines*

'A moving, humane, often funny no...... instances of heroism that can save a life…Darrieuessecq champions an ordinary, powerless individual, who proves herself nonetheless capable, now and again, of doing good things that, without saving the world, can reduce the suffering of another individual. What would we have done if we were Rose? Or rather: what are we doing?' *Les Inrockuptibles*

'No other author writes about being a mother as intensely and as precisely as Marie Darrieussecq…This is the story of a woman asking herself how she can be in some way honourable in the face of the world's absurdity…Written with compassion and humour, and with no moral other than that of giving meaning to one's existence.' *Elle*

'There's nothing particularly heroic about Rose. She won't save the world. She has neither the soul nor the courage of a revolutionary. But on this night of chaos and confusion on board a cruise ship, she has the instinct to help a young Nigerian refugee. She does it without a second thought…*Crossed Lines* is a work of consciousness-raising about the controversial issue of refugees. It is a bet with humanity, proof of the need for active resistance. "We can be heroes, just for one day."' *Le Soir*

'Rose is Madame Everywoman, an appealing character, a woman of her time, a mother through and through, funny and full of life, just like the writing in this novel, a wonderfully humorous, spirited and thoughtful book.' *Le Point*

'Rather than moralising, *Crossed Lines* reflects the confusion and helplessness of our society in the face of refugees on our doorstep. Darrieussecq admits to feeling the same degree of goodwill and awkwardness as her protagonist, without any solution to offer. "That confusion and distress is everywhere in my writing."' *Lire*

'*Crossed Lines* is a wonderful novel, one of those books that never leaves you, which you remember with absolute clarity. It is a perfect work of fiction, giving you the happy sensation of recognition…A novel is only successful if it makes the universe dovetail with the bedroom (or the dining room). This is true with *Crossed Lines*: what space or place are we able to offer in our lives for someone who has none? In the end, this is a novel about adoption.' *Charlie Hebdo*

'Rose is an ordinary woman, positive and endearing, full of life, who ends up saving her marriage because she knows how to look beyond her own perspective. *Crossed Lines* rings true from the first page to the last and leaves a lasting impression.' *Femina*

'Darrieussecq's perspective is neither one of pathos nor of resolution. Her strength is to relay, on the one hand, the point of view of a middle-class family with existential bruises, a bit messed up, a bit alcoholic, also in migration—from their unsustainable life in Paris to the town of Clèves in the Basque country—and, on the other hand, Rose's fumbling attempts to come to grips with an enormous contemporary issue. Our issue, refugees. In stylistically perfect realism imbued with touches of irony and philosophical depth, *Crossed Lines* manages brilliantly to steer a course between the self and the world.' *Libération*

'Working with stereotypes and clichés has always been a pleasure for Marie Darrieussecq. In *Crossed Lines*, Rose is a loving wife and mother, worried about the viability of her marriage. She's also the archetypal Parisian thinking of moving to the country. And she's a worried, helpless spectator of those who are less fortunate than her. In this novel we see a woman transform her everyday life in order to rescue a child who is not her own.' *Télérama*

'A wonderfully astute novel that succeeds in bringing humour and apparent simplicity to the serious themes it deals with. In her spare prose, Darrieussecq recounts Rose's thoughts, her feelings and her doubts, and at the same time she evokes the background noise of our time, and the things that remain unsaid—all with an ironic gaze that is never cynical.' *Le Monde*

'*Crossed Lines* is not a bleak, moralising tale. It's mischievous, witty, not the slightest bit tedious. "The truth is," says Marie Darrieussecq, "I met quite a few refugees who were in good spirits." At the risk of shocking those for whom refugeedom is exposure to extortion, rape, torture or death, the author has no hesitation in describing "young men heading off on an adventure". No, Darrieusseq does not dwell in the domain of the politically correct: "I write to disturb readers."' *L'Obs*

'Marie Darrieussecq reads the testament of Modersohn-Becker— the letters, the diaries, and above all the paintings—with a burning intelligence and a fierce hold on what it meant and means to be a woman and an artist.' J. M. Coetzee on *Being Here: the Life of Paula Modersohn-Becker*

'*Being Here* is a luminous tale about the courage of the lone female artist.' Joan London

'Poetic and poignant…*Being Here* positively quivers with life.' *Sydney Morning Herald*

'The issue of otherness is crucial, as is that of the couple. Are the characters a couple, or are they just the sum of one another? This novel and its romance is a surprise from Marie Darrieussecq, but she proves herself to be, as ever, a socially-aware writer.' *Paris Match* on *Men*

'*Tom Is Dead* is powerful; when one has finished reading it one feels it absolutely needed to exist.' Nancy Huston

'Darrieussecq doesn't so much write words; she's a gale prising them out from where they hide...She drags you into a vortex of "after", where the words "mourning" and "grief" are pounded into something less than ash...If you take the time to follow her into the vortex you'll be returned to the commonplace world enlarged and admiring of a writer who forces language to go beyond itself to reconsider the ancient idea of being "mad with grief".' *Age* on *Tom Is Dead*

'Darrieussecq evokes the awe, fear and weirdness of motherhood, the demolition of certainty, an instinct for rapture. She puts her hand in the great dark lake of maternal experience and scoops up filigrees of the phosphorescent memory all mothers share, turns them gleaming in the light of her words, one after another. I was disturbed, envious, enthralled.' Kate Holden on *The Baby*

'Vintage Darrieussecq: tender, disturbing and indelible.' Chloe Hooper on *The Baby*

'There are few writers who may have changed my perception of the world, but Darrieussecq is one of them.' *The Times*

'The internationally celebrated author who illuminates those parts of life other writers cannot or do not want to reach.' *Independent*

MARIE DARRIEUSSECQ was born in Bayonne in 1969 and is recognised as one of the leading voices of contemporary French literature. Her first novel, *Pig Tales*, was translated into thirty-five languages. She has written more than twenty books. Text has published *Tom Is Dead*, *All the Way*, *Men*, *Being Here: The Life of Paula Modersohn-Becker*, *Our Life in the Forest*, *The Baby* and *Crossed Lines*. In 2013 Marie Darrieussecq was awarded the Prix Médicis and the Prix des Prix for her novel *Men*. She has written art criticism and journalism for a number of publications, including *Libération* and *Charlie Hebdo,* and is also a translator from English and has practised as a psychoanalyst. She lives in Paris.

PENNY HUESTON has translated five other books by Marie Darrieussecq, as well as novels by Patrick Modiano, Raphaël Jerusalmy, Sarah Cohen-Scali and Emmanuelle Pagano. She has been shortlisted for the JQ-Wingate Prize, the Scott Moncrief Prize, and twice for the New South Wales Premier's Translation Prize.

Translated from
the French by
Penny Hueston

MARIE DARRIEUSSECQ

Crossed Lines

TEXT PUBLISHING MELBOURNE AUSTRALIA

textpublishing.com.au

The Text Publishing Company
Swann House, 22 William Street, Melbourne Victoria 3000, Australia

The Text Publishing Company (UK) Ltd
130 Wood Street, London EC2V 6DL, United Kingdom

Originally published in France under the title *La mer à l'envers* by Paris, 2019
Published by The Text Publishing Company, 2020

Book design by Jessica Horrocks
Cover photo by Ali Harper/Stocksy
Typeset in Granjon 13.75/19.5 by J&M Typesetting

Printed and bound in Australia by Griffin Press, part of Ovato, an accredited ISO/ NZS 14001:2004 Environmental Management System printer.

ISBN: 9781911231349 (paperback)
ISBN: 9781925923568 (ebook)

A catalogue record for this book is available from the National Library of Australia.

For Paul

'We can be heroes,
just for one day.'

DAVID BOWIE
Heroes

It was her mother who convinced Rose to go on the cruise. A way of getting some perspective on things. Of thinking about her marriage, her profession, moving house. Go away with just the kids. Have a change of air. The Mediterranean. For a girl from the Atlantic, it's flat. A small sea. The coasts not that far apart. It looks as if Africa is pushing headlong into Europe, which is probably true in any case. A tectonic sea, destined to close up.

For the time being, the area is large enough to be able to go on a cruise. But not too huge either: the speed of this enormous cruise ship amazes her. The propellers are producing huge white bubbles beneath the dining room. The wake spools like a ribbon. Stromboli rears up over the water: a red glow on the summit of a black triangle. And the cloud sitting above it is not a cloud but smoke. There are volcanoes in the real world. There really is lava that has come from deep in the Earth. And all of it not so far from where she lives.

'You're ignoring what you have in your hands—you have a gift.' That's what her husband said to her. For a long time, she acted as if it didn't exist, this thing she could do with her hands. It was even a bit grubby. And then this cruise came along. An opportunity that lasted for only a second. A second that she had in her hands, that she held there, a fragment of time, still pulsating.

Younès—the hero of the story, in her eyes—was her witness. And she feels as if she's his witness.

I

'There was not a single person in
the whole audience who was not
overcome, carried away, lifted out
of himself by the speaker's words!'

JULES VERNE
From the Earth to the Moon

Something woke Rose that night. A *tap tap*, a different sound from the motors. The cabin was floating in the blue. The children were asleep. From her bunk it was difficult to work out the motion of the ship. She was inside it—on board—but she might as well have been trying to feel the rotation of the Earth. She and her two children must weigh not much more than a hundred kilos of living matter among hundreds of thousands of tonnes. Their cabin was located on the fifth of twelve decks on the three-hundred-metre-long vessel that housed four thousand human beings.

She could hear shouting. Cries for help? Commands? Or was it the clanking of chains? What time was it? Three in the morning. She couldn't see anything out the porthole: the wrinkled surface of the sea, opaque, unpleasant. The black sky. The Deluxe cabin (that is, economy class) didn't have a balcony (the Prestige and the Nirvana cabins were not in her mother's price range—the trip was her Christmas present to them), and without a balcony you couldn't see a thing.

She adjusted her daughter's doona, then stood there for a minute. The cabin was dark, cosy, but the burst of noise warped the space around her. She opened the door onto the corridor. A man from the Comfort cabins (in the middle, without portholes) was looking at her as she stood in front of her open door. She was wearing a respectable pair of pyjamas, over which she had thrown a long woollen cardigan. He was wearing a pair of designer trousers and a palm-tree-print shirt. From above came the sound of rapid footsteps and people shouting in Italian. The passenger opposite turned towards the lifts. She hesitated—the children—but when she heard the lift ding she followed him.

They went down without speaking. There was ambient music. Perhaps it would have been smarter to go up, towards the bridge and the commanding officers? Unless the problem was to be found below, in the hold with the machines? The ship seemed to be digging a hole in the water, thrusting down as it struck the surface, asking questions in the search for a way through.

The lift doors opened onto cigarette smoke and blaring music. A décor of pyramids, pharaohs and sarcophagus-shaped lamps. Girls in gold lamé were perched on stools. Elderly men were talking and laughing in various European languages. The guy from the Comfort cabins went into the cognac bar. Uncertain, she stood at the intersection between two musical zones: three black guys in red-and-white outfits, playing jazz, and an Italian singer with curly blond hair, accompanied by a pianist on a rotating podium.

Holding her breath, she crossed the smoke-filled casino. Which direction was she walking in? Port was smoking and starboard non-smoking. Or was it the other way around—she could never remember. The casino was under the waterline. The players coalesced like piles of seaweed around the tables. She wanted a glass of champagne or any sort of cocktail, like the girls in gold lamé. A very old couple were shouting at each other in Spanish while a scarcely younger woman was grabbing their hands to stop them from hitting each other —*que lucha la vida*—trying to get someone to back her up, Rose perhaps, who was sidestepping away.

She would have liked to catch sight of an official, one of those guys in uniform who set out the benches for the passengers on the deck. She crossed a buffet area: pizzas, hamburgers and chips, the smell mingling with the tobacco and perfume and whatever it was, a slight juddering, something vibrating, that made her feel a bit sick. The package her mother had purchased was all-inclusive-without-alcohol.

Through the bowels of the ship was another games room, for video games this time, full of teenagers up late. Then there were empty corridors, boutiques that were shut, Egyptian décor in lilac and pink, and the huge staircase in fake marble leading to the Scheherazade nightclub. Over the music she could hear noise in the distance, but when she tried to distinguish the sounds she couldn't hear it anymore.

She hesitated again. A cluster of drunk retirees was tottering at the bottom of the stairs. She visualised her little body standing up in the hollow of the massive ship, the sea below, enormous, indifferent. The passengers on the *Titanic* also took a while to work out what was going on. This trip was a Christmas special offer, perhaps because one of the company's ships had sunk a few years ago, thirty-two dead. Going on a cruise had its risks.

No pasa nada, niente, nothing, said the official in a cap, *everything's fine, tutto bene*. She felt a bit stupid but sort of alluring in her body-hugging woollens. The pool was closed but lit up. The fountain in the shape of a mermaid had been switched off with her mouth wide open. There was no doubt about the juddering when she looked at the square of pool water: it was moving in circles. The ship was treading water. She grabbed a tartan rug from a chaise longue and walked through a double security door towards the upper deck. The wind funnelled down into her and she wrapped the rug around her head. The Milky Way was frothing above her. She was an astronaut ready for zero gravity.

There was a shoreline in the distance. Italy? Malta? Greece? Surely not Libya. She had checked on the internet: a very long time from now, at the rate of a few millimetres of annual 'convergence', the Mediterranean would look like a river. You'd be able to cross it by foot (except, by then, there'd be no human beings left). Greece, the Peloponnese, is sliding down to Africa, like a big drip falling. Athens and Alexandria will be one and the same, she thinks, drowned or buried.

Cruises induce daydreaming (when you don't spend the whole time in the casino). You feel stunned, lulled. Rose sheltered from the wind under a large funnel. There was a rippling of lights on the deep black horizon. Once again there came the sound of chains—can a ship this size drop anchor anywhere, or what, just drift? She shuddered to think how cold the sea must be at this time of year. Someone in a yellow oilskin was running towards her in a racket of heavy steps on the metal bridge.

'Is it...?' she asked, but he'd gone past, his walkie-talkie crackling away. The bridge was silent again. She could see her shadow in the glow of the Christmas fairy lights, a huge round head on a stick body. It was freezing. Do astronauts contemplating the shape of the Earth feel as if they alone are in charge of the world?

Right. Rose went back to her cabin. The children were asleep. She put on her jeans, a warm jacket and her sneakers. She checked that her son's mobile was turned on: 4.02 a.m. She took the life jackets out of the wardrobe, the small one for Emma, the big one for Gabriel, and placed them on their bunk beds. They looked like two big fluoro security blankets. She imagined herself at home with the children, and Christian, her husband, their father. That familiar sensation of suffocation beneath her sternum. She took a photo, without using the flash, of her splendid children, asleep, one above the other against the golden background of the Deluxe cabin.

On the twelfth and top deck, she reached the ship's prow, with views out over both sides. To get there she'd had to go through the rollerblade rink and the children's games plaza, and skirt the swimming pool, the outdoor one that was covered with a net at night. She was getting her bearings. And now all she had to do was follow the sounds. Voices, screams, yes, tears? The ship was motionless over the black depths. She leaned forward. There was a suicide on every cruise. The ships leave with four thousand on board, and how many do they return with?

A fixed yellow spot shone in the distance—how far away? She went down a walkway, another one: a dead end. Back through the double security door towards the centre of the ship, a wide, warm hallway, in the Prestige section, more room between the doors. She stepped over room-service trays left out on the carpet, found another double security door and emerged onto a gangway in the wind. A 3D puzzle.

Down below, underneath her, they were putting a lifeboat into the water. *Rat-tat-tat* went the chains. The lifeboat got smaller and smaller, the surface of the sea seen from above as if from an apartment block. Silence. Like red scratches, the noises split the night. An official and two sailors descended the length of the ship wall in the lifeboat, a big pile of life jackets at their feet. In the sea there were what looked like effervescent tablets, spume. She could hear screams. And she could just make out another boat, smaller but still sizeable. Holding her hand up against the Christmas lights, her eyes growing accustomed to the night, she connected the noises to the actions and worked out that the crew members were saving people.

Some other passengers on the parapet were trying to look too. It was the two French couples from Montauban she had met briefly in the Deluxe restaurant. They said hello to her; they were drunk. The two women, young, were tripping around in high heels. 'They're going to be at it for hours,' said one of them. One of the men shouted at the other woman, 'Holy fuck, you're a dentist like me!' Which made them laugh for no reason.

Another couple was running towards them, wearing sneakers and tracksuits. Jogging at this hour of the night? They were speaking a language she didn't recognise. Scandinavians? Rose tried to explain to them in her high-school English that there were people down there in the water. And little by little, as if in response to some kind of mysterious message passed between them, other passengers joined them. What time was it now, half-past four in the morning?

The lifeboat had reached the water, knocking against the side of the cruise ship. Watched by the passengers leaning over the railings, its motor started up smoothly, the officer at the bow and the two sailors behind, standing very straight, as if in a painting. Other life rafts were being readied for descent. She wondered whether she should go and wake the children so they could watch.

A member of staff appeared: 'Ladies and gentlemen, please go back to your cabins.'

Gradually, amid the sound of motors, the life rafts drew away. The voices seemed to be walking on the water. In various different languages, passengers were asking what was going on, even though it was obvious. *Why aren't they calling the cops? It's up to the maritime police to intervene. Those people are crazy—they take children with them. All the same, we can't let them drown.* It was one of the Frenchwomen who said this, and Rose felt a rush of love for her honourable compatriot.

An officer was saying again, in English and in Italian, that everyone had to leave the bridge. The drunk French dentists said they were cold and the swell made them want to throw up. 'Come on, let's have one last drink,' said one of the dentists. Rose stayed with the honourable Frenchwoman while the other woman ran off after the men, her ankles in a twist.

Rose couldn't see a thing. No moon. It was too hazy to make out the stars and impossible to see beyond the ship's own illumination—a gigantic glow of floodlights and fairy lights. The electric backlighting made it difficult to focus on the sea: the only thing visible was the disturbance not far off, the whitened surface and the fluoro dots of the lifeboats rocking in the water. The bright yellow spots remained on her retinas and masked what Rose was trying to see; she had to close her eyes and open them again, but the imprints of the lights kept dancing in her vision, like an annoying, flickering Christmas display.

Please, *prego, signore, i passaggeri devono tornare alle cabine…*

Encouraged by the other Frenchwoman standing firm in her high heels, Rose stayed where she was. The officer tackled another group, his arms outspread as if they were a herd of animals. Down below on the first deck, a crowd of company uniforms was bustling around—sailors or staff, she could never tell them apart. Someone was talking into a megaphone, in who knows what language. Syllables were bouncing off the water like bullets. With the yellow dots of the lifeboats it was like a giant tennis match, but on the wash of the sea.

More uniformed staff appeared, insisting the passengers return to their cabins. She and the honourable Frenchwoman slipped through a double security door into a lilac and golden universe smelling of sausages and Shalimar. The vast heat of the ship carried them like a belch to the other side: *bloob*, they popped out, recharged by the heat and animated by the music, desperately curious and already keeling over.

They set off back around the ship, cutting through by the swimming pool, where they grabbed piles of tartan rugs in the company's colours. Loaded up, they made their way to the bottom deck, where the action was, where the sea was close by but still below them, where earlier, group by group, all the passengers had gone through evacuation drills, and where now the manoeuvres were for real. The two women saw that while they had been circumnavigating the ship events had unfolded: the boat in distress was now clearly visible, a sort of little trawler with a tiny cabin and completely crowded with people, even on the roof of the cabin, piled up, squashed on top of each other, all calling out the same thing.

Despite the efforts of the crew, a lot of passengers had gathered together again to watch. Somewhere on the cruise ship she could hear an out-of-tune chorus singing 'Happy Birthday'.

Was that a volcano, or dawn breaking? But they were in the depths of winter, so if it was broad daylight anywhere right now it would be in Australia.

And down there in the sea, was that someone swimming? How could anyone swim in that position? Or was it a subterranean swimmer, doing freestyle beneath the Earth's crust, between enormous pits of lava and clay, and emerging here on a blind guess, stunned?

He was dead. They were in the process of fishing his body out of the water, there, right below, a dead man.

A death, just like that; a sudden death. The lifeboat crew were trying to perform CPR on the man, but it was clear they were doing it without much conviction: a man who's alive doesn't hold his head like that. She felt the reflex to hold out her hand to them, to try to do something, but…

She placed all the rugs at her feet. She had carried them here for those who might be cold, for the living. She and the honourable Frenchwoman stood there, speechless. Seeing a dead person with someone you've only just met creates a sudden intimacy. Rose's hands were firing with unused energy. She had never seen a dead person, apart from her grandmother in the village funeral parlour. She had a vision of herself in the passage of time, the seconds spinning past, at the end of a huge funnel, a vortex viewed from the stars, with this woman who meant nothing to her, and this dead person: she knew that she and the woman who meant nothing to her would remember this precise moment, this dawning 24th of December, for the rest of their lives.

o

Get a grip. Stay calm. She was issuing herself commands in the same tone as the crew members. It was time for her to climb down from her mental hyperspace and return to the deck. Find out where things were at. The little trawler was about to make contact with the cruise ship. *Bump.* The honourable Frenchwoman was leaning over the railing, calling out. She should mind her own business. Rose could make out much smaller shapes on the trawler in distress: babes in arms.

Thumping sounds were coming from the enormous ship; it was snorting like a large animal biding its time. The crew were stopping the boat people from climbing aboard headlong—the deck was too high for them. Women and children first, like in the movies. It took Rose a while to grasp that they were trying to get the people to climb into the lifeboats first, then—imagine an elevator—to hoist the lifeboats up the side of the cruise ship. The sailors were hooking up chains, like on construction sites when the crane operators prepare heavy loads. The chains tightened. The oval shape of a lifeboat loomed large, full of round heads. But one chain ratcheted faster than the other; there was screaming; the lifeboat lurched, then righted itself with a sharp yank, almost tipping over. What a manoeuvre! Then slowly the oval lifeboat loomed even larger, emerging above the kitchens in the lower closed deck, the sea just below it rising and falling, until the crew tied the boat to the first deck. They made it, the lifeboat full of hoodies and beanies and sodden scalps.

A man stood up, holding out a small child, the first child, to a chain of arms, the sailors safeguarding the transfer. The child was taken by one sailor, who passed it to another, who placed it in the arms of the Frenchwoman, who was calling out. You'd have thought it was her child, that she'd been waiting for it and it was now being returned to her. Her head bent over it, she talked to the child, wrapping it up, her evening dress already soaked. But more children were arriving, and still more, some scarcely bigger, some walking, and Rose was suddenly overcome by what was happening, all these drenched children, numb, alive, snatched from the sea, the precise equivalent of death.

The crew were yelling; a different momentum was underway; they were being driven backwards. Her new friend from Montauban was heading off with another group. Suddenly Rose understood what she'd been shouting: *Doctor—I'm a doctor*. Other passengers were rushing onto the deck, all with the same dumbfounded expression. Everyone was pushing and shoving, the boat people climbing up one after the other and the passengers coming down to see—as if they were made of different materials, one lot soaking, the other lot dry.

Now it was the women who were being rescued, all very young and all shivering. Rose was about to pick up the rugs and offer them around, when there was a burst of brightness on the ground: an explosion of golden-yellow emergency blankets unfurling, the large folds throwing into relief the outlines of the women, who were sitting down, collapsing into the rustling material. But the men from the crew, all in oilskins, got them back on their feet and led them away. There were *thank-yous* and *mercis* and tears and exhausted murmurings.

Then the men arrived, or rather the boys, neither children nor men. A black hand grabbed her by the sleeve and fingertips grazed the palm of her hand, and there was that thing, the tremor, *bang*, the shock-wave that seemed to tear away a tiny piece of time.

But she doesn't have time, right now, to think about that tremor; she sees his eyes and a request: water. The international language of the hand cupped towards the mouth. Her panicked brain comes up with a jumble of too many solutions: the whole cruise ship is flowing with mineral water, still or sparkling, tea, coffee, fizzy drinks, juice, beer, alcohol of all sorts, and in her own cabin a range of drinks, including water from the taps in the bathroom, but by the time she got there, he'd have been better off following the crew members.

He is very young, wet curly hair, a large, uneven forehead. He looks like her son. She says to herself: if I adopted a child, it would be him. When you adopt, apparently that's what it's like: immediate recognition. Or perhaps any old kid asking her for water looks like her son? She moves away from him—there'll be water over there, over where they're taking them; it'll be warm and there'll be food. Over there, she points: follow them.

And she turned towards the sea—something was approaching. Another lifeboat, but only two men aboard. Two men standing up in blue and yellow oilskins, and a glistening wet pile—a heap—how many bodies? She looked around for her Frenchwoman or other living people—she was being jostled again and almost trod on a body laid out on a rug. That's the dead man, she said to herself, her first death. She stepped over the body.

Where were they putting them? That was the last lifeboat. Patches of bright red floated in the water, along with life jackets washed this way by the waves. Where was her friend, her friend the *doctor*? Had she seen the lifeboat full of dead bodies? Or was she clutching onto the children for something to do, a mission? Was she hiding her head in the children's hair?

Rose followed the passengers; the enormous, warm, musical container of the ship wrapped around her again. For the second time that night, she returned to her cabin.

The children were asleep. It was 6.12 a.m. She packed away the life jackets. She sat down. It was hot. A shower. That's it: a shower.

She needs to feel a jolt, she needs to feel something reliable. It seems to her as if she's guilty. Her, Rose Goyenetche. Who would not harm a fly. Surely her name would be way down the bottom on the list of guilty people? She touches the inside of her palms, trying to find that thing she has in her hands, her strength, but it never happens when she's by herself. The hot water is gushing out, the soap making bubbles between her fingers, hot water from the

world of luxury, cold water transformed at an astronomical cost into hot water and running out of the
plughole into the sea.

She studies the hollow beneath her sternum. It's
beating. She's alive. She visualises the pile of dead
bodies in the lifeboat and the boy who is thirsty, and
she feels the electric shock of their contact and she
visualises Christian, her husband. The two images
aren't connected. Divorce and rescue. Her marriage
and, what, migration. There is as much difference
between the living and the dead as between the warm
interior of the ship and the frozen dinghy out there.
She soaps her body and the images lather up. She sees
young men in sodden clothes knocking on the doors
of her childhood, on the painted doors of the village,
asking for work, for whatever, for a euro an hour
they'll clip the hedge, pick fruit, wash the floors, wipe
old people's bums, relieve aches and pains, and do
repairs. The euro hadn't been introduced back then.

She turns off the taps, steps into the muggy heat
of the bathroom. The cabin is a fishbowl of tepid air;
it's easy to imagine it suddenly filled with a whirl-
pool of saltwater, she and her two mangled children
thudding around like a load of laundry in a wash-
ing-machine drum. They must have taken the

boat people to where the Filipinos, the Peruvians, the Indonesians sleep—the staff who maintain the ship, provide the wait service and make up the rooms. In the hold. Obviously they're not going to put them in with the passengers.

Gabriel reaches out to grab his phone. His big curly head rises as he looks at the screen, his face pale blue, then he burrows back under the bedding again. The porthole. It's not light yet. The circle of the sea and the sky, cut in half, is metallic grey and steel blue. *Mum*, says her son. She sits down. She strokes the soft hair on top of his forehead: he's fifteen, he's five. She is right here, right now, so much so that she's choking on it—this love that's bigger than space. A love that contains the world. *Where are you going?* He falls back to sleep.

Six thirty-three. Still another half-hour before the breakfast buffet opens, but coffee is available from various self-serve stations. She gets the thermos from the bottom of their excursion daypack. Rinses it. Takes a pair of her son's jeans and one of his sweaters—not the cashmere one, the wool-blend one. And a pair of boxer shorts, a T-shirt, socks. She hesitates over the parka: Gabriel will need it. The rain jacket, then. No. The parka. Anyway, it's getting too small for him. She stuffs it all in the backpack. There. Now everything seems urgent.

Under the emergency blankets, the new arrivals look as if they're in sarcophagi, wrapped up and lying in a line, as if for transporting, and the crew seems bent on arranging them so that they take up the least possible space. Other staff have appeared, deck washers and housekeeping guys. She recognises the Peruvian waiter she talks to in Spanish in the restaurant. They're in the process of shutting the double security doors. How many of these doors are there on each level? Could you disappear on the ship, like a mouse? My wet hair from the shower gives me a bit of a disguise, she says to herself as she grabs one of the emergency blankets; what is she doing?

She is in the area below the waterline, beneath the casino. How deep is this ship? It's the staff quarters. A large group of rescued people are sitting or lying down in a big, brightly lit, steamy assembly room. She sidles through them; *sorry, excuse me*—a large young woman in a tight-fitting wet tracksuit was not moving aside, boys were sitting with their hands on their knees, some of those lying down were asleep, a group of women were wearing heavy veils that seemed to rise from the floor to cradle the babies. It was as if she had to invent a new form of politeness or a new steadfastness in order to slide her body among these bodies, these layers, these sodden piles, sweatshirts, tunics, sweaters, caps, tracksuits, hoodies. They all smelled of the sea and of diesel. There was the strong stench of fish, as if they'd been hauled, streaming with water, from the maw of the monster. From the ship's kitchens, there was also the aroma of the metres-long trail of pizza that was being handed out to them.

It was raining in the room, condensation dripping from the ceiling. He was looking at her. She had trouble recognising him. Like when two babies have been swapped at birth. The same straight nose, the same colour, the same curly hair, but almost dry now, shorter. He looked away. A few crumbs of pizza in the corner of his mouth. And his forehead? She thought she remembered an uneven forehead, like babies who've been left with forceps marks. It was him. The boy to whom she hadn't given water. He was waiting, his eyes like two blades. They were all waiting (except the ones who were wiped out—they were asleep). They weren't talking, as if they knew how to wait (she didn't know how to, she said to herself). They were waiting without any control over the situation, none at all, none of those crucial details that determine a future (she said this to herself too).

She sat down next to him and handed him the thermos and the bag of clothes. He said something to her that she didn't understand. Thank you, probably. With a quick nod of his head that she couldn't decipher, his eyes lowered: shy, cold, humble, resigned, a nice kid, polite, exhausted. He was missing two or three front teeth—not his baby teeth, surely? He held onto the thermos and stopped moving. So she'd struck a klutz? She took the thermos back, poured some coffee into the cup for him, placed it in his hand and for the second time felt the slight tremor, and he felt it too. He drank and he murmured the same thing again. He pulled a strange face and she realised that she should have added sugar; he'd drunk the bitter stuff out of politeness. He clasped the unopened bag of clothes against his body. She offered the thermos around.

'I'm sorry,' she said to no one in particular. 'I forgot to put sugar in the coffee. Sorry.'

The large woman in the wet tracksuit took the thermos and it disappeared, passed from hand to hand with more murmurs. His eyes were still lowered; Rose was smiling, for want of anything better to do. She would have liked him to look at her. There they were, like two idiots. Near the back of the room a man in a white lab coat, the ship's doctor, looking completely overwhelmed—gerontology was normally his thing—was grasping the hand of each person, one by one, with both of his hands. He was wearing latex gloves—she understood why, because she'd once had a case of scabies in a young male patient. Roughly two hundred people, two hundred hands. She withdrew her own hands instinctively.

The honourable Frenchwoman was in another corner. She'd put on a white coat too. That's what Rose needed, something official. There were two crew members with iPads, taking down names and heading in her direction. They'd picked her for a passenger straightaway. She gave them her name anyway, 'Rose Goyenetche, psychologist', but they kept on with their job and moved to the next person. It wasn't just her skin that set her apart from the crowd, as there were a few pale faces among the ship-wrecked group; it was her overall appearance, the spanking-new look about her whole being. Whereas the boat people had something worn-out about them, as if their shape—seated, lying down, crouching, or even standing up—their faces, their hands, their clothes, their expressions, the drops of water running off them, as if everything about them was somehow heading forward, but was at every point blocked, impeded, ground down, held back.

Next…it was him. His name was Younès: she heard Youssef, no, Younès. He also told them his surname, but she couldn't make it out. The two officials wrote it down and went on to the big woman in the tracksuit. Younès said something that ended in *mobile phone*. She held out hers to him. No. From his pocket he took out a sealed ziplock bag—at home she puts grated carrot in them—containing a mobile. An old Samsung with a cracked screen. It wasn't turning on, or rather it was turning on—he showed her, the battery wasn't the problem—but nothing was happening. She could see droplets beneath the screen.

She is not a repairer of mobile phones. She holds out hers again; they both peer down at the screen; other heads crane forward, the big woman in the tracksuit and others. Her phone is working, of course—7.19 a.m.—but there's no network. They're too far from the coast. There's wifi on board, but she didn't purchase that package, too expensive; she just uses her phone plan's data. Well, she's not about to explain that to them.

He tells her, in French, that he needs a phone. He doesn't make eye contact with her as he speaks; he looks into the middle distance. The large young woman in the tracksuit interrupts them in a strident voice, in a language Rose doesn't recognise but that includes some English words pronounced with a harsh accent. 'She is Nigeria,' he says in a slightly disdainful tone.

In Rose's set of stereotypes, the box marked *Nigeria* is empty. She thinks he's got a nerve, in the state he's in, all soaking-wet sixty kilos of him, to consign the woman to a lower rung of sodden boat people. And to ask Rose for a phone. She stands up, because she's got an idea. She starts speaking to him in the same affectionate tone of authority she uses with her son. He should stay there, wait for her (as if he was going to go anywhere). She uses 'tu' when she addresses him because he's how old? Sixteen. She steps over the bodies; at least these ones are all alive, she says to herself. Someone stops her—oh, her thermos! They give it back to her. It's empty; she experiences a feeling of sheer contentment.

o

For the third time that night Rose returns to her cabin. It's now 7.31 a.m. She washes her hands. The children are still asleep. The whole cabin, which she keeps rediscovering, seems to her to be incredibly comfortable. She leans over Gabriel. Buried in the doona and pillows, in the warm pyjamas she insists he wears. His perfect golden gossamer hair. Above him, in a cloud of white bedding, is Emma. Her son's mobile phone is half-hidden under the pillow. She takes it.

Five unopened messages. What would be the least inconsiderate thing to do? Make a note of them to tell him later? Send them to herself so he can read them on her phone? Or nothing? She has never read any message that was not addressed to her. It's a point of honour for her. Not her husband's, or her son's, or anyone's. Even though she knows all the passwords, because they're always losing everything—she runs the whole house, the phone plans, the phones, the washing machine, the dishwasher, the shopping, the holidays, the house-moving: everything.

She gives her son's phone to Younès and tells him the passcode. She also gives him the charger, because that's common sense, and she has a lot of common sense. When their hands make contact there's the little electrical *ping* she was expecting. She smiles at him; he looks serious, not exactly serious, more like focused, even curious: he's going to talk to her about it, she says to herself, about the power of that current between them. She's ready to explain that sometimes it's embarrassing, but that it happens to her with other people as well. But, come on, she's just given him a phone. He starts examining it.

The large young Nigerian woman has put on Gabriel's wool-blend sweater. That's annoying. But, after all, if the girl needs it…She's bulging out of it. Two breasts like watermelons. Not the most appropriate sweater.

Younès has opened up the phone. His SIM card doesn't work. A bit of tomato sauce glistens on his upper lip. She wants to wipe it off, but restrains herself; it irritates her son when she does things like that.

There's a disturbance in the back of the room, a noise; some of them have stood up, others are still asleep—they were being given some information, or orders, she couldn't work it out, but those whose eyes were still open were all staring in the same direction. And that vision of them there, some standing up nervously, some collapsed on the floor, imprinted itself on her retinas with the power of a painting. Several officials were urging them to move. Younès looked at her: she gestured for him to keep the phone, she nodded, yes. He crept away. He was tall, a lot taller than her son, but now she could no longer see his figure in the milling crowd.

They were silent. A man was speaking. In English. The ship's captain. The day before he had posed for a photo with her daughter. He was young yet had a craggy face, blond but sturdy. He had a trendy beard but was an old *sea dog*. He had honoured the Kids Club with a visit, and *snap*, the ship's photographer had *immortalised the moment*. But the man talking was no longer playing to the gallery in his white uniform; he was talking rescue services, medical care, a speedboat from the Italian coastguard. His words were greeted by a commotion, a storm of exclamations. 'In Italy,' the captain repeated. The voices calmed down, some of the exclamations were joyful, some people were crying.

She wondered whether the bodies had been put in the ship's morgue. Whose bodies were they? Had Younès lost someone? Did they send the dead bodies away, and if so how far? *Women and children first.*

She felt called. That fundamental sentence. That inevitable sentence. She stood up, dizzy, black dots dancing in front of her eyes. She thought about those glimmering fluoro spots, far away, drifting away, drops of exploded mercury in a thermometer, separated or reunited depending on chance events.

She had heard about the Englishman who had tried to hide a little Afghan girl in his car so that she could be reunited with her family. One article described how the Englishman's wife had left him while he was living in the refugee camp in Calais. But now that the camp had been evacuated, had his wife taken him back? Or was he persevering, hiding with the others in the dunes and bushes? She wondered fleetingly if he drank, like her own husband. What sort of husband was he? And the captain, what sort of husband was he? What a life it must be when you're the big-hearted, long-haul captain. Was he the same at sea as he was at home?

Everyone had stood up, the women, the children and the men, the conquerors and the stranded, and, as they did so, Rose had a vision of the painting *The Raft of the Medusa*, the human tide of bodies, tilting; they were all focused on a single point over there—the captain, hope and, behind him, a corridor, Europe.

But suddenly there were dings all over the room, chirping, whistling, snatches of songs, ringing and buzzing, as if all the drops of condensation were falling from the ceiling. Everyone was hunching over. Rectangles of blue light appeared beneath faces. The network. They were approaching a coastline. Everyone on the raft of the Medusa was looking at their phone. For Rose there was just a single text, from her husband: 'I miss you.' 8.38 a.m. She called her son's phone, and what does she hear from the end of the room? 'IT'S YOUR OLD LADY CALLING YOU, BUDDY, IT'S YOUR OLD LADY CALLING YOU.'

Her son's stupid ringtone. Obviously. She hung up, flustered. And she located Younès. There he was: above the heads, his broad forehead, his youthful face lit up by the phone. He thrust the phone into his pocket and looked up at the captain. He was off on an adventure. He had got through the hardest part of the journey. He was leaving, off to his future. The captain was shouting instructions. And if the captain had felt the vibration of a call in his pocket too, he made no sign of it. Right now he was continuing to steer the ship and the world.

o

Her son had tipped the mattress and doona upside down and yanked his clothes inside out. 'It'll turn up.' The words she used for all the lost soft toys and keys and glasses and public-transport passes and wallets and phones. Calming, maternal, conjugal words. Words that warded off bad luck. And the things always (almost always) turned up. He took her phone out of her hand to call his. He'd wanted to call himself with his sister's phone, the little Nokia, but it wasn't charged. No ringtone sounded in the cabin, nor in the bathroom—and yet Gabriel had a clear memory of his phone not being on silent. She lifted up a few pillows for form's sake. She needed a coffee. Emma was whining that she was hungry.

There were too many people in the cafeteria, and still no phone. 'I had it during the night!' her son moaned. They ventured into the restaurant. As luck would have it, they found a table, near the picture window, and while she drank and nibbled on almonds and fruit (her own fair-trade organic almonds that she carried with her by the kilo—her husband jokingly called her *my squirrel*), Emma piled up croissants and pancakes and waffles and dough-nuts and Nutella and maple syrup. Rose cut up bananas and peeled apples, none of which they ate, so she ate them. Her son was getting annoyed with her phone, trying in vain to get a signal: without wifi it was impossible. She told him off because now her screen was sticky with Nutella.

It occurred to her that she was happier than she had been for months. She was even perfectly happy. Her children were wonderful. The colour of the sea was royal blue. The sky too. And there was nothing else to see. A watery planet whirling in the sky.

Gabriel went back to the cabin to keep searching. She couldn't help making a snide remark about his addiction. He retorted furiously that he'd been making notes.

Notes, what for?

Just notes. Forget it!

She and Emma set off to stroll around the ship. They had plenty of time before Kids Club opened for the day. The older passengers were circulating in the area like arthritic lobsters: in dressing-gowns towards the saunas, in bathing suits towards the pools, in sportswear towards the gym, in smart casual wear, evening wear, beach clothes or whatever for those who were going down to the casino. In the shopping arcade she stopped in front of the photographer's window: there they were in a picture, her daughter and the captain. Ten euros. Her little girl hugged the print against her heart and Rose had to take it back from her: she'd damage it at Kids Club.

'I don't want to go to Kids Club,' said Emma.

'You don't have a choice,' said Rose. 'I'm on holidays.'

The captain was as handsome in the photograph as he was in person. She dropped the sobbing Emma off at the club and headed to the ship's administration centre. She booked the obligatory excursion to the Parthenon and took out a wifi subscription for the remaining days of the cruise. She owed her son that much. She rang her husband. And after that, finally, she would have a rest.

His voice sounded strained but normal. Ten o'clock in the morning. He was sober. He was on his way to yet another site visit at rue d'Aboukir. And he launched straight into a rant about his boss and his whole good-for-nothing team. 'You're going to get burned out,' she told him. And he'd received an outrageous invoice for the renovations of their house in Clèves. It was a lot to manage, the construction site, their upcoming house move, all the unsellable apartments his boss was palming off onto him on the pretext that he was the best real-estate agent. 'You're burned out,' she said again. But he wasn't listening. He hadn't listened for months, years. If she said to him, 'I'm leaving you,' would he hear her?

She settled into a chaise longue alongside the picture window. She could hear the pool water sloshing behind her. The invoice was for the bathroom, for the laying of those little tiles she had chosen, those *really* little tiles—she held the phone away from her ear a bit. Passengers in white bathrobes were looking, as she was, at the sea. It felt like a health spa.

'Gabriel can't find his phone,' she said, to change the subject. Her husband snorted: they were not about to buy him *another* one. 'But you know what they're like without their phones. They'd rather die than not have a phone. They'd rather be without a dick.'

'Have you tried Lost Property?' said her husband.

She stood up to get herself a coffee. In her earphones Christian was still speaking. She wondered how he would cope if she left him. She would not let him speak to her like that, in that vaguely friendly way, unburdening himself in order to seek strength and solutions to his problems.

Listening, listening…No, she would no longer be a sounding board for him. The coffee was just bitter-tasting water. Espressos were not included in the 'all-inclusive' package. How do you arrange a meeting place out at sea? At a fixed point, at the intersection of such and such a latitude and longitude? Or did the two ships head towards each other? Which was faster? Her husband was speaking to her from rue d'Aboukir now, he had arrived in front of number 44; and she couldn't make out the shoreline, only a line slicing through the blue, light blue at the top, dark blue at the bottom, the same colour tones that Ulysses must have gazed at.

She decided to go to the bar at the stern to look at the wake and to buy an espresso. So: for the time being, this was the goal she was setting herself. The bar was called the Miramar and the décor was inspired by the nineteenth-century Greek Revival style, with square-shaped frieze features.

Number 44 rue d'Aboukir was unsellable because a widely reported murder had taken place there. The door and windows behind which Veronika L. had been imprisoned, raped and killed had featured on TV. A tortured tenant and a cursed apartment. No one wanted to handle the file, not only in the real-estate agency, but in the whole company and perhaps the whole city. A pool of blood.

The owners, a harmless old couple, had had everything renovated, at their expense, of course—you can never expect any assistance for that kind of thing. Her husband had found a trauma-cleaning service. The team arrives kitted out like astronauts, they remove what can't be cleaned, clean what can't be removed, until the apartment looks like a water-logged wasteland after a fire. Ground zero. It was all they owned. The tenant had been financing their old age. And now their plans were in tatters.

Her husband even found them a psychologist, one of Rose's colleagues. Oh, she knew her husband well: he wanted to *save* that poor old couple. This morning he was meeting an engineer from Total Nigeria, the type of guy in a hurry who has a lot of cash and no time to lose on human-interest stories. The ideal pied-à-terre for a single expat guy. Right in the heart of the Montorgueil neighbourhood, on the top floor.

The wake was magnificent. A perfectly steady rhythm, swelling like two lips. Rose waited in front of a picture window, leaning against the sea, occasionally looking out for the waiter, here he comes, her espresso on a tray. She wished good luck to her husband, who was being waved at by the Nigerian engineer at the end of the street, and contemplated the boat people several decks below her, who were waiting. She drank her excellent Italian espresso. On the map of her mind, the two boats, the cruise ship and the coastguard speedboat, were two blinking dots converging. The Mediterranean was a sort of sea lion with a long snout pointed in the direction of Gibraltar, the Balearic Islands were like eyes, Corsica and Sardinia were ears, Sicily a fin. Hovering above was Veronika L. Below were the boat people.

All of a sudden she saw her son entering the bar. It looked like he was on the phone, his head lowered. Yes, he was talking on the phone, what a jerk, his sister's little Nokia, when she was on cheap plan, it was going to cost a fortune. He got off the phone when he saw her. 'I'm walking round the whole ship, calling myself,' he explained. 'I'll end up hearing my phone somehow. It'll ring, it's not on silent.' He was red in the face, out of breath.

'What's the ringtone when your sister calls you?' He looked relieved that she was taking his problem seriously. 'IT'S YOUR BIG FAT SISTA CALLING.' He imitated the nasal voice of the ringtone. She wondered how Younès would cope with a phone that kept saying 'IT'S YOUR BIG FAT

SISTA CALLING.' She hoped he'd put it on silent.

'Emma's not fat,' she said.

'It's just an expression,' said her son.

She asked him if he wanted something to drink: a Coke. He was jittery, muttering about his notes, the thing he was writing, it would be terrible if he lost it…She told him that she'd signed on for the wifi package, that they'd find all his data, that in most cases nothing is ever lost. That they wouldn't say anything to Dad, but at the next stopover she'd find out where to buy him a new iPhone, especially as they weren't expensive in Greece and on a cruise shopping was duty-free.

Through the window she could see the Italian coastguard's speedboat. White and red. Her son had taken her phone and was trying to connect to the wifi, frenetically keying in his passwords. He stood up, knocking over his Coke. 'There it is,' he said. He pointed towards the back of the room, down the ship. She was wiping up the drink with serviettes, a waiter rushed over, replaced the Coke, as her son showed her on the screen where his phone was—right here, on the ship. A blue dot was pulsating in the grid of lines, close to the red dot that marked their location. Her son zoomed in and out: the app was sluggish—the blue dot looked as if it was a few metres from them, but it was zigzagging in fits and starts. He was *below them*, thought Rose. Her son made a beeline for the door, holding the screen out flat in front of him like a compass.

'Wait for me,' she called. 'Wait for me! Hey, that's *my* phone!'

The speedboat had drawn alongside the ship. A large crowd of passengers was helping with the manoeuvre, adjusting fenders and throwing ropes. But they could no longer get down to the lower deck: the migrants had been rounded up there and all the double security doors had been shut. Rose was looking for Younès among the heads she could see from above. The children and a few women were in a little group to the side. He was no longer a child and not yet a man. Where was he? She was too high up. The passengers were all speaking at once in all their different languages. Like choreographed pink flamingos, they were filming with their phones, their arms held out towards the speedboat then drawn back in, taking selfies, lengthening and shortening the focus. They were smoking, tweeting, drinking coffee.

One hundred and fifty migrants from West

Africa, plus a dozen Sudanese, a few Eritreans and, no one knew why, two Vietnamese.

The sun was warm. It was nearly midday. No wind. It was extraordinarily beautiful weather, the sky was cloudless: the Mediterranean at Christmas.

Opinions were divided. The enormous bubble of commentary swelled like steam, filtered up through people's hair and dispersed in the blue sky. Not all the poverty in the world, no, but a portion of it. They've got a choice—look, they're all black, it's not a war, it's not Syria. What would you know about it; have you heard what's going on in Eritrea? Do you even know if the borders are open or shut?

Rose felt valves opening and shutting inside her, the clacks and pings of a pinball machine. And, once again, she visualised her home town, God knows why these pictures appeared in her mind, like post-cards. The town square was rearranged. There were the roundabouts, the inn in front of the pelota court and the cemetery with round headstones and the nineteenth-century church and the multimedia library and the kindergarten and the primary school and the car park between the two, and, right in the middle, all one hundred or so foreigners, in tents. Or? Or what if every resident in the village took in one foreigner. Down there, deep in the south-west, far from anywhere, in those huge houses and those empty holiday houses. It's perfectly logical to share the planet in a better way, but in Clèves? Right where she was moving precisely in order to get some peace? She looked around for the honourable Frenchwoman but couldn't see her.

Her son's neck was twisted and his fingers were hooked around the screen of the phone, her phone. She rubbed his back. If he could just relax, take in his surroundings. The sea. The migrants. The crowd. The blue sky. The world. Tell her what he thinks about it. If he could just think about it, anything at all. And when he does, if he could tell her what to do and what to think.

But she realised he was calling, yet again, the number of his damn lost phone, tapping Gabriel in Contacts, and she was worried it would ring down-stairs, on the deck where the boat people were, broadcasting the horrible ringtone, 'IT'S YOUR OLD LADY CALLING YOU, BUDDY'. But all she could hear were the boats bumping against each other, the speedboat that seemed so tiny, scraping the enormous wall of the cruise ship, and the sea breaking between the two, sucking and spurting, a terrifying natural phenomenon. No one wanted to fall in there. She held her son by the sleeve as she looked for Younès. There was no ringing sound, no words reaching them, apart from commands and cries of protest, and silence, the silence of waiting.

They were climbing into the speedboat. Assisted by the crew and all wearing life jackets. It was orderly. But she couldn't see much. On the roller-blade rink, right up high, there was a small patio area in full sunshine, with a few—what are they called?—spyglasses or telescopes.

She was not the only one to have the idea. She waited her turn behind a line of passengers. And when she pressed her eyes up to the—binoculars?—her son said, 'That's so gross. It's *voyeuristic*.' She was pointing the binoculars in the direction of the heads moving laboriously, in turn, from one boat to the other, from the big boat to the little boat, via the bottleneck of a gangway that had been cordoned off. She couldn't see Younès. She was trying to think what the scene reminded her of.

There was some kind of agitation, congestion, one of the heads wanted to go ahead of another. Then the flow improved. It was like looking through a microscope, red blood cells progressing through veins, constricting, sticking together, separating, struggling for life. She had a flash of the dead person she'd stepped over in the night. And the lifeboat with the two sailors standing up. She raised her head and the sky erupted onto her retinas. Her pupils contracted. If her son could just look, if he could just see, if he could just tell her. There they were, both of them passing so close to wars and disasters, two drifters on the surface of the planet. Her son's future would be bleaker than her own, she was certain of that. But not as bleak as that of Younès. In all probability and according to the statistics. The problem with migrants is how upsetting they are.

The speedboat was drawing away. The cruiseship passengers were shouting goodbye, bon voyage. A few of the boat people waved back. It was kind of cheerful. The speedboat accelerated while the ship reignited its gas turbines, if that's what you call them on a boat; in any case the vibration became much stronger, they were setting off again.

'It's them!' yelled Gabriel. On the phone's GPS the blue dot was moving away from the red dot. The little blue pulsating dot, symbolising his phone, was *leaving* the cruise ship, moving away, through the sea, into an empty grid pattern.

'My phone! It's them!' her son screamed again. 'Them, those guys, on the other boat! They stole my phone!' She turned her head towards the sun. How wonderful was this gentle, warm wind on this planet unevenly covered by water. Twenty degrees on a winter's morning. Balmy even. One more thing to worry about—the climate.

She put another euro in the binoculars, followed the speedboat for a second, then made a big sweep of the sea. Not far away was another little boat that seemed to be observing the whole scene. On the hull was painted a large eye, like you see in Turkey, or Egypt, or, who knows, in Libya, with an Arab inscription. The eye was watching her. How idiotic.

'They're going off with my phone!' her incredulous son continued. He needed her to deny it, to reassure him, like when children want you to say, what a nice wolf, and anyway he's not real. She looked at her son through the binoculars. He was enormous and out of focus: a large pink-and-yellow mass split into two, shaking. He wanted another version, a fairytale or the truth. He was fifteen.

But she had to go and collect Emma from Kids Club; it was almost lunchtime. Now Gabriel was trying to work out how they'd done it, how they'd got into the cabin, those invisible, shifty, mercurial guys, at what time exactly did they rifle through his things, haunt his corner of the cabin, bewitch his possessions. They'd even taken his charger, he couldn't find that either.

At least she knew now that Younès had definitely boarded the speedboat.

They got to lunch late and chose the Escapade set menu—hers was sole fillet and mixed salad, lasagna for Emma, and for Gabriel a crumbed veal cutlet that he didn't touch. It was so annoying watching him torture himself over that phone.

'I'm really not that keen on the way you call the boat people thieves,' she said. 'Besides, you should say refugees, or people in exile.'

'Oh, for God's sake,' said her son.

'What do you mean, for God's sake, didn't you see how much they were suffering? Why not call them immigrants like we used to, and let them stay here for a bit?'

Rose was getting irritated, her son too.

'You're so ridiculous with all your middle-class leftist crap.'

'What?'

In any case, he'd managed to retrieve his precious notes from the cloud, and his contacts.

'But what are the notes for?' asked his mother, trying to calm down. 'Come on, we're on a cruise, we're on holidays.'

They were running late for their scheduled arrival in Katakolo. An official was going from table to table reassuring the passengers that the excursion to Olympia would definitely go ahead, only it would be slightly shorter, or those who no longer wished to go would be reimbursed. Thinking of their school curriculum, she would have liked her children to see Olympia, but she'd got up so early, she was exhausted, and then the day after tomorrow they were going to the Parthenon anyway...

Were Gabriel's notes for a school assignment?

A French couple was complaining: it's Christmas Eve tonight, what time would we be getting back? She had forgotten. Emma had not forgotten.

Emma had asked a waiter for a piece of paper and was writing her umpteenth letter to Father Christmas: mauve-coloured rollerblades (the ones they hired on the rink were *boys'* rollerblades), the cruise-ship Playmobil with the boat, and also the pirate Playmobil, a loom for weaving friendship bracelets, especially in

Brazilian colours…Each word had to be spelled out for her: she was still in Grade Two.

'You'd be better off drawing pictures,' said Rose.

Gabriel called the waiter over to ask for the dessert menu.

'But you haven't eaten your cutlet,' said Rose.

Emma asked how to spell *My Sims Get Famous*.

'Draw it!' shouted Rose.

'But it's a Nintendo game,' wailed Emma.

'So draw a square,' said Gabriel. He grabbed her crayon and drew a large square on the letter to Father Christmas and Emma started crying and Rose exploded, then apologised to the smiling waiter, who said to her in Spanish that he had an identical little girl at home, exactly the same adorable little girl, and, as he placed two cigarette wafers in Emma's ice-cream, he showed Rose a photo of a little Inca girl on his phone, two black plaits and an aquiline nose. She didn't look anything like Emma. Rose admired the photo. She was embarrassed by Gabriel's bad-mannered indifference, but she felt dizzy with tiredness. She'd been awake since four.

She stood up, told Gabriel to take his sister back to Kids Club, and went upstairs, or downstairs, she no longer knew which it was, to her Prestige cabin.

o

The cabin had been made up. It was such a pleasure to slide naked into a big bed with clean, tightly tucked sheets in the middle of the afternoon. She glanced out the porthole. No building opposite, obviously. It was a Parisian reflex. And, even if a boat went past, who would be able to spot her minuscule shape in among the hundreds of openings? A floating apartment block, her husband had said as he flicked through the brochure. But it was more than an apartment block. It was an ideal city, utopia for those with walking frames. There was a doctor on board. And a priest. Some seniors preferred cruises, at a thousand euros a week, to retirement homes. She could picture them, senile and sailing far from the tumultuous shores, dying at sea in the cotton wool of luxury liners, like pinned butterflies, on an acid ocean, alongside submerged coastlines from where climate refugees were migrating.

After their own cruise, the ship was setting off on a world tour for four months, the very same ship. Gabriel and Emma were dazzled by the idea. Marseilles, Dubai, the Maldives, Australia, Tahiti, Hawaii, Panama and the Antilles, let's go. There would be a few children on board, with private tutors—Rose had to explain what they were.

She was curled up, her elbows close to her body, nestled in, a bubble beneath the sheet. A powerful mechanism was carrying the ship forward as it made up for the delay. She pictured the propellers…A retirement home on propellers…She had already lived a whole day and a whole life. She saw a small boat approaching; a man stood at the back, steering. A volcano loomed on the horizon. The small boat was coming towards her, for her—she woke with a start.

What time was it? She reached for her phone and remembered that she'd lent it to her son. The cabin seemed full to overflowing with a strange fluid. She could still feel the movement in her legs, in her hips, from when she'd stepped over the body. This morning she'd stepped over a dead body. So that she didn't walk on top of him. Even the idea that she could have walked on top of him…The contact, the idea of the contact.

Again, she had the impulse to reach for her phone. She could call her husband. Set foot in the world again. On solid ground. Or Solange, chat with her best friend. What happened last night was not part of her life. She had to pull herself together, reconnect. Come on, get a grip. Perhaps it was also the bizarre effect the holiday was having on her. It had been so long since she'd gone away on holiday. The effect of leaving. As soon as the cruise ship had weighed anchor, she had not given work another thought. At all. The cruise effect was instant: a confrontation with the sea, braving the elements. She turned to look out the porthole. They had docked. The quay was empty. The sun had set.

Surely Gabriel wouldn't have got off the ship by himself? He would have needed his boarding pass to get onto dry land and there it was on the table with Emma's pass. She got dressed. Where were they? Emma's phone was almost dead, where was the charger? This must be Greece. Katakolo, for sure.

Father Christmas was at Kids Club. Emma, face painted as a cat, had received some presents, which she showed Rose, one by one: the cap with the company crest, the cruise-ship keyring with the company crest, the plastic thing to make bubbles with the company crest and a ball-thrower, also with said crest. Beneath Father Christmas's beard was one of the club's activity leaders, Hamid, who had sort of come on to her the day before. She borrowed his phone.

Gabriel was in the gym. Stay there, she told him,

she was on her way. Dad called you at least twenty times, he said.

Emma the cat had a big red scratch across her forehead. Father Christmas explained to Rose that they had screened *Bambi* in Italian since most of the children at Kids Club were Italian, right, the others spoke English or German and there were English subtitles for the ones who knew how to read. Anyway, Emma, the only French child, started crying and they couldn't work out if it was because of the death of Bambi's mother or that she couldn't understand anything. Anyway (at this point in the story Rose felt her daughter's sticky little hand wiggling in hers to say, no, no, that's not what happened), an Italian child, actually two children, a brother and a sister, gave Emma a little bit of a scratch because her crying was obviously stopping them from hearing the film.

'They called me a bloody French girl,' bleated Emma.

So the language barrier was not insurmountable. The little hand was still trying to communicate her own version of the facts into Rose's hand, a current running between daughter and mother, demanding, urgent, so exhausting.

She bought her an ice-cream. That wasn't so difficult.

The cruise ship was quiet. She liked the stop-overs: the ship emptied. She hadn't set foot in Barcelona. Nor Rome: what could she possibly do in ten hours, four of which were in a bus? Look at the fortifications of Valetta from above? But Athens, all the same, that was a must: they'd do the Parthenon. Tomorrow. Just the idea of it wore her out.

Emma, however, was in top form, her regimen of ice-creams and sea air was doing her good. She was running through the corridors: not an oldie in sight. Run, Emma, run! The emptiness was having a euphoric effect on them. The sound of her little feet on the carpet died away, Emma disappeared round the corner; the corridor seemed deserted. *Boo!* She sprang out. Each time they found each other again, they leaped for joy. Her daughter in her arms, laughing ecstatically, madly, as intensely as she had been crying twenty minutes earlier. Alive, they were all alive. She was going to find her son. She was going to call her husband. She would ask herself again whether she should leave him, perhaps, but she was alive.

Gabriel was on a treadmill facing Greece. He looked as handsome as a young god. Without stopping, he handed back her phone. The battery was almost dead. She saw that he'd erased the history. She got a bit of a shock when she thought about everything she'd have to pay for that wasn't included in her contract.

She called her husband: We're in Katakolo, in Greece…She listened to him telling her—quickly, I don't have much battery left, she could hear the familiar sound of the bottle and the glass, it was only five in the afternoon—that the engineer from Total turned up with his Nigerian fiancée, he wasn't single at all, she was amazing, a bombshell, like a princess, an apparition, skinny, red nails, red lips, a dress, one of those dresses that crosses over, yes, a wraparound, she looked at everything with contempt, I thought she'd blow the whole deal, and then in the end it was cash up front, no mortgage, nothing, maybe she's the one paying, so we're meeting next week at the lawyers, they'd never heard of Veronika L., or else they couldn't give a damn. But, added her husband, I still think the whole murder thing is a real downer.

She could visualise him, in his windowless office, the door shut while he drank and spoke to his wife, to tell her, listen, that cruise is fine, but come home soon. Then he would put away the bottle and open the door again to his idiot boss and his incompetent agents, and then he'd dash to the Montparnasse station and take the train to Clèves and supervise the work on their house down there…

Emma wanted to have a go on the treadmill too, in her socks, not too fast, Emma, please, not too faaasst. Like a good brother, Gabriel had his arms around her and was laughing. Greece was undulating in the picture window. The empty gym on the top floor overlooked the world. Every single sporty person on board must be doing Olympia. The news was on the television, turned down. Rihanna was the very loud sound on the sound system. On the screen, pieces of twisted metal were strewn across the orange ground, along with bits of bodies, and running along the bottom were words and numbers and definitely the word Nigeria.

She persuaded the children that they should get off the ship and go for a wander in Greece before the Christmas banquet. And what about a new iPhone for Gabriel? That made up his mind. They beeped their passes at the ship's exit. Immediately they were struck by how motionless the ground was. Their bodies were pitching, it was land sickness. As soon as they disembarked, ten or so musicians dressed in fustanellas and pompom shoes began furiously playing the sirtaki, and two women danced frenetically in the cold.

They had to walk for a long way in the shadow of the cruise ship, the wind carving out a glacial corridor along the specially constructed seawall. At the end of the block of shadow, the sun was setting. More locals in traditional dress were handing out ouzo in front of the duty-free shop, thank you. The children had yet another fruit juice. Emma was having fun feeling herself moving without moving, the sea still in her legs even though everything was upright, it was all about balance, the inner ear, the spirit level at the back of the ear.

Gabriel was standing in front of countless iPhones. She had given Younès an iPhone 5. The difference in price was astronomical. Wouldn't a Samsung be enough for an adolescent? But, come on, it was Christmas. And tax-free. She got a bottle of Chanel Chance for her mother and yet another Barbie for Emma. What about something for Christian? She hesitated. The whisky was a bargain. Single malt was his favourite. 'Should I get some whisky for Dad?' All of a sudden she really needed help. But Gabriel was champing at the bit to get to the checkout. The blond archangel wasn't answering. To drink or not to drink. Little white houses lined up along the wharf all the way to a grey beach. There was a cafe and a few souvenir shops. Emma wanted an Olympic Games magnet and Gabriel wanted a case for his new mobile; unfortunately they'd have to buy the SIM card in France. Until then she'd lend him hers. And they'd also have to change the phone contract. And the number.

'The number?' He gasped.

'But I'm paying for the new—bigger and better—contract.'

'With, like, unlimited credit?'

Like.

He put on a Happy Christmas face. She also bought him a sweater because it really was chilly. Winter was catching up with them.

Emma didn't want to go back to Kids Club and said her Barbie was *crap*; she wanted a *real* phone too, with Facebook and everything. Gabriel told her she was too little, and for Facebook too. Emma burst into tears. It wasn't clear whether it was out of anger with her brother or having to wait so long, or what. She has everything and she cries. When you think about the children in Syria, or Yemen, or almost anywhere else, especially girls.

At the double security door, she beeped their three cards with the embarkation staff and turned towards the facial-recognition camera. The enormous metal partitions swallowed them up, and here they were again among the golden wall hangings and tables of welcome drinks and the three or four smiling Peruvians standing firm in the wind, the wall hangings flapping, the tablecloths fluttering, a barrier of hot air inside pushing the cold air out and she could almost see, yes, she could actually see the two huge balloons of air, head-to-head currents, battling it out. She had to hold on to Gabriel. A dizzy spell. It's nothing. Just a long day. Come on, get a grip. She recited to herself the Buddhist saying she sometimes recommended to her patients: 'If your compassion does not include yourself, it is incomplete.'

In the cosy cabin with the evening chocolates left by the housekeeping staff, she still felt shaky. The porthole was almost black. They were still docked. She put her mobile on to charge. Gabriel was playing the *Life Is Strange* video game. 'I had another vision… The town is going to get wiped out by a tornado.'

Lying on her bed, she tried to get her bearings, the back of her head, her shoulder blades, sacrum, elbows, calves, feet…A bit of *mindfulness*. Breathe, here, now. She concentrated on the passage of air through her nostrils, breathing in, breathing out, not straining, thinking about not thinking is still thinking, words entered her mind, *that cruise is fine, but come home soon*, faces came back to her, the lifeboat full of dead people, stepping over the body, she pushed it all out of her mind, breathe in, breathe out, the words were leaving, slipping away, as were the images, her anxiety was turning into a sort of distant cloud.

She leaped to the end of her bed and demanded her SIM card back from her son. Your what? The SIM card for my phone. It was a fiddle trying to put it back in, her clumsy fingers, he helped her. She felt like downing a big glass of wine. Tonight she'd have some champagne, shit, it was Christmas. She asked him how to use geolocation tracking with her contacts. You have to go into Find My Friends. She had never used this ridiculous app. A map appeared, a grid of latitudes and longitudes. Gabriel went back to his game; he couldn't care less about her old iPhone now. She pictured the whole planet covered in mobile phones until there was no more subsoil, no more *rare earths*, and the entire crust had vitrified into something like a hardened saddle cloth.

On the screen, the map was moving by itself. It zoomed in on the Mediterranean, on Italy. On Sicily. The blue dot was pulsating. With Gabriel written above it. It seemed strange. But it was working, it meant Younès was somewhere between Catania and Syracuse. Ashore. On dry land. She studied the blue dot as if she could make out a place, people, cops… What camp? What metal gates? While she was heading away, towards Athens. She wished Younès a safe journey. She would have liked to speak to him through the little blue dot as if through a keyhole, or something, pray for him, send him some good vibes. She concentrated on his name. Younès.

As they were leaving their cabin, the door opposite, on the Comfort side, opened. The man from the night before came out; she wasn't sure whether to greet him. But he 'totally dissed her', as her son would have said. He seemed to be shifting from one foot to the other, his gaze off in the distance. It was like the guy was out of focus. As soon as his back was turned, all she could remember was the black hole of his mouth, as if he had been gasping for breath.

Perhaps the drama of the rescue had affected him? The expressions on the faces of the other passengers were as untroubled as the surface of a lake after a pebble has sunk to the bottom.

As she moved through the themed bars, she became obsessed with wanting to have a drink. She imagined herself as a flute being filled with champagne, from her feet to her knees, to her genitals, her navel. Hunger? No, she wasn't hungry. On board, everything tasted the same, an all-purpose Italian slop. The feat of filling four thousand bellies daily meant using tonnes of the same tomato sauce, which turned up, admittedly with some ingenuity, in the cheese balls, the polenta tart, the spicy prawn pasta, the turkey rolls, but not, however, in the tiramisu.

She accepted the glass of prosecco that came with every adult's Christmas meal. Straightaway, she wanted another one. She called over the waiter and flashed her boarding card, which paid for everything: a glass of real champagne. If she was going to drink, let it be the best. She wondered if her husband was as easily geolocatable as Younès. Most likely. Did people really keep tabs on each other like this? Not if you click on Ghost Mode, her son explained.

The table service was a bit shambolic due to the

late arrival of the buses from Olympia; she and the children were about to start on their Yule log just as legions of exhausted, ageing day-trippers arrived in the restaurant. The word 'refund' was being uttered in various languages; she was going to hear all about it, she was hearing all about it. Olympia is actually a long way away, not at all what they told us, and there's absolutely nothing there, *only* tourists. The dentist from Montauban wanted her to acknowledge his disappointment. She wondered if he was expecting to see the Games, faster, higher, stronger, naked sprinters, athletes in short skirts and shot-putters beneath a timeless sun. She ordered another glass of champagne. 'Mum,' said Gabriel. Mum what.

What with the olympic passengers and the background music, the noise was increasing. Soon enough Italian hits from the eighties blasted out under the Egyptian chandeliers. Emma and Gabriel were playing games on the paper placemats, using the little packet of pencils and the little torch and the little kaleidoscope, all bearing the company crest. The room was gradually filling up with this rubbish; the Earth's core had been extracted and spread on the surface and would soon suffocate all life.

The Peruvian waiter, the one with the Inca kid,

rocked up all smiles to get Emma dancing. *Torneroooò, com'è possibile, un anno senza te…* Gabriel stood up too and danced in a parodic fashion, with that irony of young Parisians, which they think is witty and which makes everyone despise them. She liked this sad song. Was the Peruvian waiter also paid to provide entertainment? Or was he dancing for pleasure, or out of sadness, missing his daughter and his home country, and because it was Christmas?

She called her husband: 'Happy Christmas!' And beckoned to the waiter. She would have been better off going straight for a bottle. Christian was in slow mode: when he knew he was drunk, he enunciated clearly. But she must be kind: no recriminations tonight, no snide remarks. Christmas. Especially as he was valiantly spending Christmas Eve in Clèves with her mother. Alcohol was so habitual for him that an area of his brain maintained operational control. And no doubt it was the very area within him— sealed, secret, stable—that still appealed to Rose. A crypt. The mystery of what was in there. Emptiness, perhaps. He was talking to her from over there, from far away. That cruise is fine, but come home. Yes, the children are fine. Emma got scratched at Kids Club. Gabriel hasn't found his phone. He's playing *Life Is*

Strange. I had a vision. The whole town is going to get wiped out by a tornado.

She could no longer hear him. The signal had dropped out. Her own booming voice was saturated with bubbles. Or everyone was calling at the same time. Christmas congestion. The only distinct sound was the clinking of bottles on glasses. The line went dead.

'*Cuando regresas al Peru?*' she asked the waiter. He filled up her glass. '*Al Peru? Soy de Filipinas.*' He was from the Philippines. Not from Peru at all. From Mindanao. She had no idea where Mindanao was. But he looked so like an Inca all he needed was a flute and a knitted hat.

'Dad sends his love,' she said to the children as they sat down again, both red in the face. Gabriel wanted to go to midnight mass.

'Oh yes,' screamed Emma, 'midnight mass!' The midnight mass was at ten o'clock. There was a note in four languages outside the little chapel: due to the number of people, the midnight mass would be celebrated in the Scheherazade nightclub. Gabriel was thrilled by the idea of going to mass in a disco.

The seniors who had arrived early to get the best seats were already sitting on the pink satin ottomans.

An altar had been erected in front of the DJ booth. Sparkling lights from the spinning balls were projected onto the mauve plush curtains. The priest arrived—a diva's entrance. He was almost as good-looking as the captain. She left Gabriel to look after Emma and went off to knock back another drink, dammit.

If it was ten o'clock when she left them, and she's done the three themed bars, skipping the cognac bar because she doesn't want to risk running into the out-of-focus guy from across the corridor…If it's, let's say, eleven o'clock, how long does a midnight mass last? The greenish depths of her mojito, full of drowned mint, look like a round ocean. And there she is on the bridge, the wind in her face, at the prow of the ship, which is running full steam ahead.

It's beautiful: the night is a swift black fluid. Her nose is freezing and her cheeks are hot. There's the Peruvian, the Filipino. Is that really him? He's being chased by a geyser. He bursts out laughing and he runs, a triple step, a dancer. Huge white spurts in the deep-black sky. It's coming from below, from the bottom of the staircase, where another Peruvian is holding a hose; they're washing the deck. The first one pushes his broom very fast, like in that Canadian sport, sliding along the wet floor, laughing. The other one wipes in a zigzag motion. She bursts out laughing. The two guys stop. What a pity! She'd like the sliding and playing to keep going. She'd like to play with them. He recognises her. Perhaps. They must work insane shifts, doing all sorts of work at all times of the day or night, different jobs, on different levels of the ship.

'Keep going!' she shouts, *continua*—how do you say keep going in Spanish? Or in Filipino?

'We hardly ever see passengers on the bridge this late,' he says.

'It's beautiful,' she replies. 'Happy Christmas! *Feliz cumpleaños!*'

He laughs. 'It's *Feliz navidad. Cumpleaños* is birthday.'

'Ah, yes. Although plenty of people are born on Christmas day.'

They laugh. He is wearing a large oilskin in the company colours, the same one all the employees wear, like the guys last night carrying the people, the bodies, on board. Perhaps he was one of those guys. She apologises for thinking he was Peruvian. There are a lot of Peruvians on board, he says amiably. And a lot of Filipinos. And Pakistanis, Indonesians…He speaks five languages, English of course, Tagalog, Cebuano (he repeats the words, laughing), Spanish, a bit of Italian, and he can figure out French.

'You figure out French?' That's a nice way of saying it. At this point, she no longer knows what language they're talking in. In Spanisholo. Thanks to the mojitos, Spanisholo is easyolo. He's nice. His colleague is going to bed. She wonders what their accommodation is like. She tells him that the man who makes up her room assured her that he was paid the minimum wage. Which makes the Filipino laugh. He's a cheerful guy. His name is Ishmael. And hers? Rose. Like a rose.

She could invite him to have a drink with her. But he probably wouldn't be allowed to. He's paid 560 euros a month. Eight months a year. But it's good work. Being a waiter is the best, for the tips, and he's also a deck-washer at night; he doesn't sleep well anyway. Ah! She doesn't sleep well either. Insomniacs always have a lot to discuss. He spends the four months on land with his daughter. In order to save money, he never gets off the ship at stopovers. He's building a house over there in Mindanao. She imagines palm trees and a house on stilts, but when he shows her the pictures on his phone it's just a cement block. He only sleeps well back home. In Mindanao. He looks out at the sea rolling past. There are salt crystals in the shape of stars on his oilskin and nostalgia in his eyes. He tells her that there are two of them per cabin and that usually they're careful about religions, but right now he's with a Pakistani who prays the whole time. Whereas he's Catholic. And tonight it's Christmas. The Pakistani is on watch duty now.

She leans her elbows on the railing. He has placed his hand on the railing. They're silent for a while. *Feliz cumpleãnos!* she says again, and laughs. He laughs. The ship is speeding along like a plane. Let's go, let's go. She's had too much to drink. She's also too rich. It would be like taking advantage of him. The difference in their economic status is horrendous. But he's strong, well-built, the same age as her, they could get together as equals, just for one night. She steps backwards, smiling. He grips his broom; I'm going to check on my children, she says. He makes a hand gesture that looks like he's blessing her, or farewelling her, or apologising.

Now she's almost running, running in the wind and the cold and the huge sea. *I had another vision. That cruise is fine, but.* Returning to the heat of the ship, inside this enormous bubble moving through the water, it feels as if the walls are folding in on top of her, a warping of metal and glass, of sea and sky, the Mediterranean like a sheet of paper from shore to shore.

It's a narrow corridor. Someone wants to get past her. There's only her and this someone here. She looks around at the swinging glass doors, the empty chaise longues, the coffee dispenser, the Egyptian wall lights, an entrance and an exit, the nowhere land of the ship, and tries to concentrate her gaze on the person. It's the man from her corridor. He's out of focus.

The nightclub is also an approximation of reality, but the altar for the mass has disappeared and a more appropriate activity has started up, a sort of tea dance. The seniors have got up from the ottomans, some to dance, others in order to let the young people sit down: exuberant sexagenarians drinking cocktails in triangular glasses. The music is thumping. She hesitates. A mojito. No, no, no. When Gabriel finds her, she's shimmying from foot to foot. She sees him and she feels like kissing him. She sees herself seeing him. She sees herself, small and stumbling and still sexy and wanting to lean on her tall, handsome boy.

'Mum...' he says. Emma's there too, asleep on an ottoman like a little old lady.

Emma wakes up very early. She wants to unwrap her presents. Rose locks her in the bathroom, with strict instructions not to come out. 'Turn on the liiiighttt!' screams Emma.

Rose has a migraine. She climbs on the bed to reach the suitcase on the top shelf. She pulls on the handle but the castors jam. Here we go: now she's put her back out. She feels like crying. She yanks the case, which falls, wakes Gabriel, who goes straight back to sleep. Emma calls from the bathroom. 'Mum?'

Aspirin. And a coffee, a coffee. She looks around for the thermos—she always keeps some in there. She gets out all the parcels, places them on the carpet, and unfolds the little Christmas tree that lights up, carted all the way from Paris. It turns out it also plays music. Music that shears her right temporal lobe, and well and truly wakes up Gabriel. She opens the door to Emma, who dives on the presents, liberated at last, like Elsa from *Frozen*, singing 'Let It Go'. Gabriel laughs. He's right, this little girl is pretty funny.

Father Christmas has brought Gabriel the video game *Limbo*, a pair of Kooples jeans, grey high-top

Converses, a new Eastpak backpack for spring, a Netflix subscription (which the whole family will make the most of) and a novel he specifically wanted to read in hard copy in order to 'take notes'. His grandmother sent an envelope with 150 euros, but that'll go towards the iPhone, won't it. Emma has already put on her Snow Queen costume, tiara and gloves included, along with a magic wand. She also has the board game *Operation*, which Gabriel will enjoy too; a pair of very cute size 28 grey high-top Converses; and a picture book, *The Little Ogress and Her Lunch*. A Petit Bateau dress, a sequined handbag, a voucher for mauve rollerblades, and a few trinkets, face paint and removable tattoos. And Playmobil, but not the right ones, Emma told her too late—she didn't buy the pirates, or the cruise ship, what an idiot, she should have thought of it. She bought her the veterinary clinic instead.

Voilà. The cabin is chock-a-block with stuff, torn wrapping paper and gift ribbon. With what? Gift ribbon. Can we call Dad? No, it's still a bit early. Some coffee, for God's sake, some coffee.

The neighbour's door was wide open, a housekeeping trolley in the entrance. She had a quick look inside the cabin. All walls and ceiling, a box with a bed and pharaoh décor, neither porthole nor balcony, neither sky nor sea, how could you survive in there? No wonder the neighbour was always wandering around outside. The housekeeping guy emerged from the mini-bathroom. 'I was looking for him,' Rose said to justify her presence, realising that it was true. The housekeeping guy, supposedly on the minimum wage, looked as if he wanted to say something, then changed his mind and polished the doorknob.

Coffee. Call her husband. It was painful to get going, to establish, second by second, a fleeting present and a muddled past. The immediate future was a hangover. This evening they'd be in Piraeus. The enormous sea was sliding beneath the ship. She had got Emma dressed for Kids Club but the little girl was claiming tearfully that she had promised, yesterday. Promised what? Never to send her to Kids Club again. What was she going to do with her all day long? She gave Gabriel ten euros to babysit his sister until lunchtime at least, then wrapped herself up and lay on a deckchair out of the wind. Sunshine. The empty blue sea. *Torneroooò, com'è possibile, un anno senza te...* It's easy to do nothing on train trips. Even easier on a ship.

o

She heard a phone ringing. She no longer had a clue where she was at with the phones. Hers, Emma's little one, Gabriel's new one, and Younès's phone, which used to be Gabriel's. The name Solange appeared on her screen. Her best friend was probably calling to wish her happy Christmas or to tell her about her latest romantic disasters. Solange lived in Los Angeles and thought she was a star. She'd leave that for later. Right now she had a migraine. What else was there to do but go with the flow?

Passengers were prowling around her. They stared at the bow of the ship, then moved away in the cold. A lot of them were killing time between meals by walking, 300 metres one way, 300 metres back, shady side, sunny side, port side, starboard, some of them trotting along, others hitched to walking frames. She thought she saw a rowboat, or were they lifeboats? Whatever it was disappeared. She had specks in her vision. There was still a good two hours before lunch, but she couldn't manage to doze off. She could have read the paper on the internet now that she'd paid for wifi. But getting online would mean downloading her emails—not now, no.

The bow's huge spume kept billowing, over and

over, its own thing, neither water nor air. Frothing but moving forward, heaving above the water while also hollowing it out—strange. If you looked at it from high above, vertically, you'd fall in. Without the railing, you'd fall in.

There were things in the water. Shapes, still. Again, a surge of unrest went through the ship, transmitted from passenger to passenger like a choreographed electrical current. No, not another boat with people? Not in the spume? The word 'dolphins' bubbled up. And now she saw them. She could see the dolphins. Their gleaming fins, their extraordinary suppleness. Their neoprene bodies in the spume. Leaping was how they swam. Ten or so dolphins enjoying the difference between them and the ship, actually spouting about the difference, speeding in a fabulous neck-and-neck race. She had the urge to call her children. But by the time they got themselves here…So many marvellous things to see. And, anyway, by the time the other passengers gathered round, the surfing mammals had disappeared.

There were 196 messages in her inbox. She had received the password to the new software program. It was called Cervix. Some of her colleagues had already used it, and she was copied into several complaints and objections—apparently the thing was dysfunctional. DIM, the Department of Medical Information, was responding to the uproar by offering a training session. But you had to connect to the software in order to register for the training session (a session, which, according to the next email, turned out to be compulsory). She could feel that familiar sensation of agitation flaring up in her chest, let's call it stress. Especially since Grichka's mother—yet another one who communicates only by email, despite Rose's advice—has rescheduled her son's appointment, not an unusual thing in itself, but she's moved it into the past, the beginning of December, why not the beginning of August while you're at it. And other patients less in need (other parents of patients) also wanted to change their appointments, in the future this time, as it should be, but writing in such a fanciful style or in such an aggressive tone that she marked them all with little flags—to attend to later. Actually, no: she collected them all in one email and forwarded it to her assistant—after all, that's what she was there for. But she immediately received an auto-reply: all appointment requests can from now on be processed through the electronic calendar downloadable through Cervix.

Rose forced herself to breathe. The air was salty. The sea was blue and indifferent.

She opened up Cervix, typed in the password, but it had to be reset by sending an email requesting a new password that then had to be personalised. She tried twice, but the Cervix webpage responded with the message 'Your registration has failed. On the third unsuccessful attempt, your access to Cervix will be blocked.' The design of the homepage was dated: a yellow background and two out-of-focus women behind a man in a lab coat.

She stood up—anyway, in order to have healthy arteries, you're supposed to move around every hour—and hid her laptop under a rug, surely no one on the ship would nick it. When she came back with a coffee, another ten emails had already arrived. She wasn't going to sort through them now, but one from her mother asked:

How's it going? The cruise good? I thought Christian seemed a bit tired guess what I saw Solange !still pretty but what a life hse here in Clèves for christmas. i want to send you some photos but I can't get them out of my memory stick you can show me how to do it.don't open emails with subject Banque de Frnace it's a virus that destroys computers.Lots of love.

Then there was the email marked 'Banque de Frnace' that her mother had managed to send her several times. Another email from DIM to remind her that the *computerised medical systems had been implemented in consultation with...* She wanted to mark all the emails from DIM as junk, but she chose to switch off her laptop instead. Switch it off and look at the sea. Yes, that was the solution, the aim, if temporary: look at the sea.

And what about Solange? So she was back in the village? For Christmas? Her friend's message was so enthusiastic that she held the phone away from her ear. Solange was cultivating (or was it natural?) the hint of an American accent. And guess who she'd had coffee with that morning? With Rose's husband, no less. The renovations on the house were stunning, bravo. Old-fashioned charm, even if it was sixties-style, you can't beat it. Are we finally going to see each other? Apparently you're on a *cruise?*

The word *cruise* came out with a slight giggle. Solange was probably drinking organic cocktails on George Clooney's environmentally sustainable yacht.

Solange would never get on board a huge ugly ship with four thousand people paying a thousand euros a week. She'd never be seen dead in one of those high-rise apartments in the ocean. But she was no doubt signing petitions to open all the borders to every destitute person in the world.

Look at the sea.

The two rabbits were looking at each other in amazement. They'd come out of the same hat, when only a second ago each was in its own box. Then they disappeared, *pouf*, inside the magician's scarf. The whole room burst into applause. Two doves flew into the air. A bewitched audience member stood stock-still on two stilts. A woman was cut in half. Emma was beside herself with joy. Gabriel was trying to see how it all worked. Rose studied the program by the light of her phone. She wasn't sure she'd stay for the next show, the Gypsy Champions, which started at ten. The magician asked in several languages for a volunteer for the next act. Clairvoyant hypnosis. Who? Emma was jumping up and down. Me! Me! Rose had trouble making out who was stepping on stage. Was it an accomplice? Or someone already hypnotised? Everyone was clapping. It was their neighbour from the cabin opposite;

he almost came into focus on stage in his bright blue suit.

Rose had already lived this scene. She had already seen the neighbour step onto the stage in his bright blue suit, seen him hold the magician's gaze then sway slightly, as if from an ocean swell. The magician said he could sense that in the man's wallet, apart from the usual cards and documents, there was a photo of his two children, aged…he hesitated…and Rose knew what he was going to say…when the photo was taken the children were fifteen and eighteen…the déjà vu unfolded inexorably…they were standing in front of an alpine landscape, their names were Klaus and Susan…in Bavaria…Rose could feel her palms getting hot. A battle was taking place between her and the magician; she didn't want him to keep going with his act, stop, stop…The man from the cabin opposite started to tremble, there you go, he was shivering inside his blue halo. His wallet appeared as if by magic in the hand of the magician, who took out the photo of Klaus and Susan in Bavaria.

'I'm very sorry,' said the magician. 'Klaus is dead, I can't see him clearly on the photo. Susan is now twenty-one.'

His words were greeted by a clamour. The man

remained silent. His outline was growing blurry. Was Rose the only person witnessing his disintegration? Her palms were aflame with helplessness.

Emma was clapping and cheering.

'We should ask him where my phone is!' said Gabriel.

She had to get out. She had to get off the ship. Rose could no longer remember when or how she had boarded, in what port, in what city, what day. She watched herself running out of the room and step-ping over bodies, but she stayed where she was, firmly on her seat, all her weight dragging her towards the bottom of the sea, with that stupid Chinese proverb going round in her head, *What is the sound of one hand clapping?*

'Rabbits on board bring bad luck,' said the dentist from Montauban, who was smoking a cigarette on the bridge. 'It's a well-founded superstition: in the past they would chew on the ropes.'

'You don't say ropes, you say *rigging*, it's the word rope that brings bad luck,' replied his colleague.

'No, it's in a house where someone has hanged himself that you can't say the word rope.'

All the lifeboats had been cleaned, stored away,

returned to their correct spots; the ropes had been coiled, the tarpaulins folded, the hanging lights extinguished, all the hulls were completely dry. As if nothing had happened. It was the evening of 25 December, and it might as well have been a dream. Rose and the two dentists nodded good night. Where was the honourable Frenchwoman, the doctor from Montauban? Rose was suddenly absolutely certain that not one of the passengers on this cruise would try to see each other again, in Montauban or anywhere else, at least not them, those who'd witnessed the events of the night.

II

'Better to be pushed to the limit than full of despair.'

THOMAS BERNHARD
Gargoyles

At 6 a.m. on 26 December, Rose woke her reluctant children. After all, they weren't going to miss out on the Acropolis. Greece was on the Year Ten curriculum, and probably on the Grade Two program as well, there's no avoiding Greece. Without the ancient civilisations, we Gauls would still be doing Celtic dancing under the mistletoe, or playing at being Basque smugglers.

She tried to rally her troops. Coffee. Hot chocolate. She would have happily stayed in bed too. She'd slept badly. Now for banishing the bad dreams. The ship was pitching more than yesterday. The only thing that cheered the children up as they disembarked was the movement of the water in the swimming pool: the swell outside had created a swell inside. The pool was overflowing, *splish splash*, from one side to the other, in a slow aquatic motion. A dozen or more Peruvians were mopping up. She thought she recognised her favourite Inca guy but now wasn't the right time for that.

The Greek coast was approaching beneath a Breton drizzle. Random cultured people pointed out the Acropolis, one of several hills beneath a baroque ray of sunshine. The Acropolis. Who would have thought that one day she'd see the Acropolis? She tried to communicate her enthusiasm to the children.

In a car park in Piraeus, in a basement filled with exhaust fumes, they waited, dazed, along with the other daytrippers in numbered groups, to get into the buses. Their francophone guide, who rolled his *r*s but was otherwise irreproachable, outlined the day's proceedings, from the Acropolis, where the Parthenon was built between 447 and 432 BC, to lunch and the return bus. She thought about her husband. They were driving through a not unattractive suburb, triangles of sea appearing between the buildings and the sky. Surely you could live here, even with the so-called crisis, if in the morning the windows opened onto this ancient, ever-changing expanse of blue and grey.

The bus let them off (she must have slept for a few minutes) in front of a little train at the bottom of a steep slope. She would have preferred to walk. She dodged the distribution of rain capes from the cruise-ship lockers. Emma struggled with hers like a young bat. To the sound of sirtaki music, the little diesel-fuelled train set off in the humid air. It didn't run on tracks but trundled through the already heavy traffic. A van pulled out in front of the imitation locomotive: the train swerved, ended up in the left lane, headed back to the right, horns honked, drivers cursed, the train accelerated to realign the carriages, there was lurching and yelling.

They made it to the bottom of the Acropolis. Emma felt sick. Rose had hoped for a strong girl, a Calamity Jane, a killer. But Emma was like the last child, the last child on Earth, she marked the end of the line of a sickly, poisoned, guilty humanity, rushing towards its sputtering extinction. Rose kept saying over and over to the children: *the Acropolis*. She couldn't believe she was going to climb it. She felt excessively, infuriatingly, excited; it got on her nerves that she was getting nervous. The actual Parthenon. Here and now. The Acropolis and the Parthenon, she was getting them mixed up, she had no idea anymore. The guide handed out entry tickets. They passed through a metal detector that beeped every single person. They had to wait while the older tourists went through. Those on walking frames stayed in a cafe at the base of the Acropolis (so the Acropolis was the hill).

The drizzle had stopped, the sun was breaking through the olive trees. Emma was hungry. Rose took out a container of fruit purée from the bottom of her bag; this kid never ate when she woke up, so of course she was bound to later. Gabriel looked at his mother and smiled. It was fleeting, in the sunshine and the olive trees. The immense joy of loving each other. They climbed the old steps, her hand clasping Emma's, who was feeling better.

'I'm going to zypnotise you,' she shouted at her brother, but Gabriel skipped ahead, then stopped to look at his phone—was he taking *notes*?

There were not that many statues. The guide was talking about Phidias. Ionic and Doric.

Huge scaffolding rose beneath the pale sky. Emma let go of her mother's hand and ran towards Gabriel. Run, Emma, run. Glowing with vitality and grace, so lively among all this petrified History, the little girl stopped for a second on top of a yellow stone.

Rose went to take a photo of her, but by the time she'd rummaged in her bag, she'd lost sight of Emma. She saw Gabriel studying his phone, but not Emma.

'Emma?' No Emma. 'Gabriel? Where's Emma?'

Emma can't be far away. She can't have evaporated in a second. Nevertheless, there's a look of concern on Gabriel's face, the hint of an emotional bond hitherto scarcely apparent. So now Rose is concerned. But, no, the child could not have disappeared in a single leap, the leap a dog or a deer might make, in that space between mother and brother, leaving her mother and catching up with her brother. And yet she is not there.

The Parthenon is there, the scaffolding is there, the columns are there. And the caryatids; there's one missing, but we know it's in the British Museum. The guide explains that the one we can see is a copy, a cast, a plaster ghost standing up there. But no Emma. Rose asks the doctor from Montauban, the honourable Frenchwoman: have you seen Emma? The woman looks at her as if she doesn't recognise her. Time is running out. Emma. Her little Nokia isn't responding. Which means nothing: the battery is never charged. Rose leaps from one block of stone to another, even in the off-limits areas. Gabriel screams: 'Emmaaaaa!'

There are people everywhere, children everywhere, and all around, circling her, eternal Athens, immense and crowded. Rose heads back to the guide. The woman has to stop talking, she has to listen.

'Emma, my daughter, she's seven, I can't find her anywhere.'

'Oh,' says the guide, 'she'll turn up.'

From that moment on, Rose falls into a time warp: it's really unpleasant, but she now has access to whatever opens up in time when one is beside oneself. She is now nothing more than a single thought: find the little girl. Did you see a little girl? *Una niña, una chica*. How do you say little girl in Greek? She can't see Gabriel now either, but he's tall, he's looking for his sister, she's counting on him. Rose catches sight of him again by the corner of the temple. Has he found her? He's empty-handed and dumbstruck. She wants to go back in time, use that magic just once, go back in time once and for all and not let go of her daughter's hand, not be okay when she breaks away. That leap, that void, that open space Emma is falling into. Every second she is not found, every second without her, is tragic. She's going to turn up. Surely. They have to stop the guided tour. Everyone has to look for her. If everyone looks, if everyone scours the hill, stone by stone, she'll turn up, surely. Archaeologically.

'Emma!'

She goes back to the guide, grabs her by the elbow: 'Please!'

'Go and look over by the little train,' says the guide. 'That's the meeting spot.'

She runs towards the little train, hurtling down the Acropolis. Are there paedophiles at the Parthenon? Statistically, yes. The driver is dozing alone in the light shining through the windscreen. Emma is not there. Rose climbs back up. She has to pass through the metal detector again; she looks for her ticket, but there's no re-entry. She negotiates: her group is up there, a little girl, a French girl, her hair in a plait, wearing a sweater with a cat printed on the front.

This is hell. She would like not to be in this day. She wants to dissolve. Go back in time, dissolved— into the mighty gastric juices of Greece, of Europe, of time and of History. She thinks about the gift she has at her fingertips, that fluid she can call on, which calms, heals, takes the heat out of things. Concentrating, she tries to release it around her, but it doesn't work; she has all this power, for nothing. She wants to lift up the Parthenon like a stone and find Emma underneath.

She runs up the Acropolis, her legs scrambling, her lungs breathing, her heart doing its heart work. She slaloms through the stones, leaping over barriers, sliding between railings, past work areas, signs about compulsory hard hats. Blocks of stone tower above her, forming labyrinths; nobody pays any attention to her; the guided tours continue below; she is so focused on searching that, every time she turns a corner, she thinks she sees Emma—outside of time, a little Athena, but nothing, no one anywhere. Emma! Emma!

There's Gabriel, his tall, thin figure. She runs towards him. The more she runs, the more it seems as if…as if Gabriel is not alone, as if there's a smaller figure. Her vision is blurry, she's going to fall.

On top of an enormous block, carved a long, long time ago by people who have been dead for a long, long time, is Emma. Gabriel is holding Emma's hand. He waves at her: he has her! They suddenly appear very distinct in the hazy sunlight. Her Nokia wasn't out of battery at all, you just had to keep trying, Gabriel brandishes his phone, and Emma brandishes hers too, she wants a *best* telephone, she wants the same one as Gabriel.

o

Four days to go after the Parthenon and she is counting them down, each night is one less night, each day brings them closer to dry land. She keeps hold of Emma. The little girl is flushed and silent from so much attention. Obviously she is no longer attending Kids Club. They will buy her a grown-up's phone. They read *We're Going on a Bear Hunt* and *I Am a Tyrannosaurus* and *Baby Butterfly*. They are snuggled up in the bunk bed under the cosy doona. They don't leave their cabin. They sing. Gabriel is allowed to do whatever he wants. They stay in bed. They eat biscuits and leave crumbs everywhere. Emma is getting more and more flushed, charged up like a battery, while Gabriel is off in the gym and Rose waits to regain solid ground.

Emma wants to go to the swimming pool and Rose says yes; she doesn't want to, but she says yes, of course. The swimming pool has reopened; she would have had it reopened just for her daughter; she would have asked her Peruvian-Filipino waiter-washer to open all the swimming pools and all the picture windows and all the ballrooms for the little girl.

There's hardly anyone there. It's raining outside and it's not warm inside. It's as if, all of a sudden, they were witnessing a break in the global warming. As if, for a moment, some cool weather was calming the general turbulence. They're in the pool and having fun diving, far away from the suicidal entropy of the world. They borrowed pink goggles from the life-guard, and in the water it's funny how you feel the ship moving, you can sort of feel the sea, you can feel yourself, how to describe it—imagine a bubble in a glass of water, you are the bubble, and the glass of water shakes. Rose is floating and holding her daughter tightly, the little body warm and alive, her skin slippery, but Rose is squeezing her so much that the kid says, 'You're hurting me.' Sometimes there is too much energy in Rose's hands.

All sorts of waters are drifting around them, carrying them, pushing against them. Rose steers Emma to the surface the way whales steer their calves with their snouts. Through her pink goggles she sees the silhouette of a man, a passenger, walking around; she thinks he looks familiar and she is gripped by something like fear. When she removes her goggles, the passenger remains out of focus, no longer pink at all but blurred by droplets of water, and he greets her ceremoniously, bowing low.

When her husband calls, Rose doesn't say a word about the out-of-focus man, because he frightens her, nor about Emma disappearing at the Parthenon, since she was found, and nothing about the migrants, of course, since that episode was so brief and no one knows what to call them anyway. In short, she doesn't recap anything for him. Everything's going fine, she says, yes, the cruise is relaxing. Her husband is heading back to Paris, leaving Clèves tomorrow, the renovations are going well, he can't wait to see them all. What a pity he didn't have enough holidays to come with them, hey.

On the last day, the ship takes off at full speed towards Marseille. The sea is rough. A lot of passengers are sick. The staff go from cabin to cabin. At the sight of the twenty-euro tip, the housekeeping attendant grants her a smile.

'Did everything go well, madam?'

It's as if he can see through her, as if he knows that she lost her daughter at the Parthenon, momentarily, of course, but as if the words *bad mother* had done the rounds in the large village that is the cruise ship.

'Everything went well, more or less,' she replies. 'No significant incidents,' she adds, in a slightly harsh tone, 'apart from the migrants, of course.'

The attendant lowers his voice and says, 'Just between you and me, we lost a passenger.'

'A passenger?'

'Yes, it happens more often than you'd think.' He nods at the door opposite, the cabins without portholes. 'People, some people, wait to be on a cruise so they can jump overboard. They're premeditated suicides. Why would you go on a cruise by yourself?'

Rose wonders if he's addressing the question to her as well, but a mother with her children is not exactly alone; no one ever sees mothers in that way.

In Paris the ground pitches a bit. As Rose suspected, going back to work at the psychology clinic on Boulevard Ornano is not without a hitch, after a ten-day cruise and a body going overboard and the momentary loss of her daughter and now having to deal with the Cervix software. There's a beep when an error message pops up. All she wants to do is write a few things in the fields, apart from the names of the patients. *Beep.* The little blue dialogue box jumps onto the screen: *It is not possible to set up a meeting in the past.* Not in the past, for God's sake, she's not Grichka's mother, she knows that time is dragging us onwards, she just wants to go back to the previous page, she wants to write, like she used to do, in the shared register: 'unable to come but called', 'unable to come but the father left a message'. Or: 'cried a lot'. Now there are only five options to click:

Register
No-show
Delete
Copy
Move

Admittedly the secretary no longer complains about having to look everywhere for the file. But when the file was passed around, people talked to each other, believe it or not. There's another beep when Rose clicks in a field.

She has to get a move on; she's late for the next patient, Bilal, a little livewire whose voice she can hear coming from the waiting-room. And then there'll be Grichka, and then Philippine, a new girl who doesn't eat, and then the 15.15 ghost who never comes, and then Danao, who is always asleep in the waiting room. Danao, for God's sake. The names they have these days.

By the time she leaves she has seen fifteen patients; she is in a bubble of words and pain and sometimes joy. On Boulevard Ornano the faces are out of focus. There's a disturbance moving through the city like a rain front. She has left work a bit out of focus too. She is struggling, yes, as best she can. Out-of-focus children clutch at her and she supports them with everything she has. And when she says the right words at the right time, some of them settle down.

Near the metro, men wearing boubous are handing out leaflets with various special offers. She is fascinated by these African holy men and their market: what they sell, what they can and cannot do. Affection rekindled, attraction guaranteed. Guaranteed contact with the spirits, sexual assistance, release from anxiety. Does it come from their hands, their eyes, their heads? Do they have that warm spot she has at the end of her fingers? Especially since they earn a better living than she does. If she ever has a go at it, it will be in her village, away from her colleagues, away from Parisians, who are not more rational than others but who prefer 'etiopathologists' to 'healers'.

Their apartment has tripled in value over the last fifteen years. The magic of Parisian real estate. Principal residence, so no capital-gains tax. They're selling before the bubble bursts. And in six months, off we go, a new life away from the capital.

As she steps down into the metro, Gabriel appears on her screen, so she answers. But it isn't Gabriel. It's Younès.

She says, 'Yes?' Even though she knows exactly who it is. She glances around as if looking for help, the entrance to the metro below her on her right, a halal butcher on her left, a Cameroonian restaurant called, you couldn't make it up, The Reunion.

'Younès.'

'Where are you?'

Where is he? Her heart is pounding. He says something. She can't hear clearly. She pictures him floating in a dark space with the *plop plop* of dripping water—she is back in the assembly room on the cruise ship. She makes an effort to visualise him better, as if her brain could geolocate him, latitude and longitude, sea, land—suddenly she realises that he's calling her 'Mum': the 'Mum' saved to the phone's contacts by Gabriel. She feels a moment of panic. Who, besides his father, his sister, his grandparents, his friends, had Gabriel put in his list of contacts?

He repeats some incomprehensible words. Was it the network, the distance, their different ways of speaking French—where was he from? Not *where was he*, but *where was he from*: she should have asked him. Back on the ship. He looked African, of course, not Syrian or Afghan, but Africa is a big place. The only thing she's sure of is that he is not from Nigeria.

She goes down into the metro. She knows that once you go three steps underground in this station, the line cuts out. Younès. A creature who appeared, *pouf*. And disappeared. She has to go home, to her children, her husband. She can't do anything more for him.

The station is a ship's assembly room. The roof is dripping. She sees all the young men wearing tracksuits with brands printed on them in large letters—Adidas, Emirates, AC Milan—and the Nigerian woman in the tight-fitting sweater and the veiled mothers and their babies. She is kneeling down in front of him, and she gives him the phone and the little bag of her son's fashionable clothes, which get passed around from hand to hand, and an extraordinary transformation occurs: the bag becomes a swag. Whatever the young men touch becomes precarious. The world loses its certainty and turns inside out like an old glove. They're searching for a safe passage, but it fills up with water, plastic debris and rags. Whereas her place on the planet has her name on it, and identity documents and something like a lifelong reservation.

In Sarajevo, a long time ago, there was that tunnel, she saw a report on the news. Food supplies, drinking water, weapons and people passed between the city and the outside world. On the Sarajevo side, the tunnel was buttressed with old scraps of wood; on the other side, the reinforcement was in metal. One of the survivors said: 'When you have not seen an apple for a year, do you hide away to eat it, or do you find a knife to share it?'

Would she have shared it? She pictures Gabriel and Emma and she sees the apple and she cuts it up in secret for them, only for them. Are all mothers cold bitches? It seems to her that, since her adolescence, the world has entered that tunnel. A tunnel descending fast, and she is in there, ferried around in her numbered cabin, her safety a completely provisional affair. She remembers what it was like before, when she didn't have children. Real heroes act by disregarding their children. Of that she is certain.

It was 7.11 p.m. and the bottle was empty. Always red. Rosé in summer in the village. Her husband, leaning on the kitchen counter, glass in hand. The saga was continuing at 44 rue d'Aboukir. He wanted the young tenant to see Rose professionally. What young tenant?

The Total engineer is renting out his new property, the real-estate agency found him a good applicant, a Swiss student, her parents are guarantors. But the student can't sleep. Guilaine, the agency's receptionist, had laughed in her face and Rose feels like laughing too. As if we're going to worry about the tenants' sleep! But the student turns up at the agency every day and Rose's husband invites her into his office and listens to her. 'Someone is watching me.' The confused tenant, who gets mixed up between real-estate agents and psychologists, who feels threatened as soon as she enters the building, as if she was going to be sucked into a black hole. The student tells him about the screaming she hears at night.

Her husband and his good heart and his bad conscience. His high-mindedness about his job, about living conditions in Paris—he's made it his personal crusade. He does battle with Paris. It's a duel between him and the city. Square metre by square metre. And the last thing he needs is ghosts.

Needless to say, he hasn't prepared a meal. Or checked on Emma's homework. It's a total mess in their two-bedroom apartment: stuff on every surface. But Rose never wanted to be like Solange, who insisted that men do things they couldn't do—in short, her friend wanted them to be women.

She's just going to lie down for a minute.

What about another man? A man who didn't drink. A more rational man. A man who was less dependent in general. A man full of life, who would carry her off in his magic cape. She thinks about their youthful conviction. In the beginning, he didn't drink. They were teenagers. He never uttered a word. He only starts talking after he's had the first drink, and he hadn't yet had that first drink. They used to listen to David Bowie. In high school. *We can be heroes, just for one day...* but they didn't know what it meant. Even when they translated it, word by word; no, they had no idea. Be heroes. Just for one day. The ceiling was spinning. Should she leave him, find the strength to leave him, would it be good to leave him, would she fall in love again, was she in love, was that what love was?

You should go away on a cruise. Yes, her mother had convinced her. Rose, who was always looking for a stable world. Sometimes she walked home from Boulevard Ornano, just so she could feel the ground beneath her feet. She was born into a conventional enough world, but perhaps it was the nature of her childhood. The same window looking out over the same landscape, the houses, all white blocks, the hedge at Solange's house. All those connections forged in the village, carried around everywhere, in the fibres of her being. And the village idiot who walked around the housing estate every day at the same time like clockwork, stuck in time, crystal clear in her memory.

Her husband, opening up the mail and looking at bills, is horrified by how much Gabriel has exceeded his phone plan. So she sits down at the computer. The courage to do these things. These boring things. In the online itemised bill she sees that Younès makes daily calls to Niger, which is definitely not Nigeria. She clicks on the 'international' option, 19.99 euros a month and unlimited 3G. It will be a sort of sponsorship; until now she's never had anything to do with humanitarian aid. Niger is at the top of the list of the poorest countries—it's the one where the women have the most children. It's poorer than Bangladesh. Poorer than Haiti. Malawi is the only other country that comes close. The shape of the country is more or less round, with the capital city, Niamey, at the handle end of a sort of spatula. Lake Chad is below, to the right, a halo of green in the desert, cracked like a windowpane by a constellation of borders. In the south there is a city with a pretty name, Zinder. And one called Maradi. The Sahara fills all the north, with oases that have other pretty names: Bilma, Dirkou, Djado, Titilibé. She wonders where in Niger he comes from.

She rustled up pasta for dinner. Now Emma is on Netflix and Gabriel is on his phone. Her husband pours himself another glass—she holds out her own glass. When he started out in real estate 8,000 francs per square metre was the price. Now it's up to 8,000 euros. It's simple: speculation and foreigners. The market is too volatile, things sell after five or six years. Her husband likes things that last: for example, when he married her, it was forever. Moving house is second on the stress scale, after grief. So he shuts the door, turns off his phone, and asks his buyers and sellers the same questions. What point in their lives are they at? Obviously he needs to know their budget, but are they more of the accumulating type or the throwing-away type? Claustrophobic or nest-building? Or squirrel-like? He wants to match the right property with the right individual. A glass roof won't be appreciated by a philistine. An internal courtyard must not be neglected. A view or no view. He gets upset. A real-estate agent is the second-most hated professional, below a banker and above a politician. The main priority for French people is to become property owners; it is also their main frustration, QED. The injustice of it all weighs heavily on him. Whereas he... He finishes off the third bottle. For him it's all about the word *inhabit*... That people feel... 'At home?' Rose finishes his sentence.

Yes. That's it. That's exactly it. He gives her a little smile. That tragic smile. With a touch of lost joy, as if joy was a flask with dregs at the bottom. 'Everything will be better in Clèves,' she says. She puts her hand on his hand. There's a weak flow of the current, yet it's not working—calming, yes, but not a cure. She probably knows him too well. A fourth glass of wine for her. Emma has to be put to bed.

Wherever you may go, no matter where you are, I never will be far away... She can hear her husband singing the lullaby in their cramped apartment. She hasn't told him about Emma disappearing on the Acropolis. No one has mentioned it. She feels as if the whole trip was made by someone else. An excursion outside her own life. Emma is there, in the stifling little bedroom, with Gabriel on the mezzanine doing who knows what on his phone. The distinct outline of Emma's little body. Her soapy warmth. Missing, all of a sudden. Among the stone blocks of the Parthenon. Replaced perhaps by a replica? Or else what? The girl who could walk through walls, through columns? A little caryatid, the world on her brow, the future on her stone head.

Younès calls back while she's seeing Grichka and his mother. It's Gabriel's blond head that appears on the screen: she still hasn't changed the photo. But it's Younès, obviously. Obviously, she can't take the call. Grichka is wearing a helmet to protect him from electromagnetic waves. Grichka is the point of contact for an extraterrestrial civilisation located somewhere in the vicinity of Alpha Centauri. He is troubled by the visits of the extraterrestrials and his mother thinks he should talk to a shrink. Grichka stares at Rose. The extraterrestrials entrust the child with particular tasks, training him for more significant missions. They communicate with him through electromagnetic waves and he finds it exhausting, hence the helmet. His mother does not want to stop the contact, simply reduce how often it happens. The extraterrestrials monitor Grichka from a distance and occasionally guide him. ('Occasionally?' repeats Rose.) Unfortunately, the mother has never seen the extraterrestrials; she does, however, feel their presence when they come near her son. Grichka is nine. The mother chose his name (Rose asked) in homage to *Time X*, the television show launched by Igor and Grichka Bogdanov.

Rose asks Grichka if he wants to say something. The little boy shakes his head, no, and some trinkets attached to the helmet wobble. The jingling of the trinkets reminds Rose of the vague interference in her head produced by Younès's phone call.

Yes, the mother understands: she has to let Grichka have some private time with the shrink. Before she leaves she rearranges a few of the trinkets on the helmet, as if they were antennae. Then they can hear her standing behind the door. Rose opens the door, takes the mother into the waiting room, comes back, shuts the door.

Grichka and Rose look at each other.

'It mustn't be easy,' says Rose.

The little boy shakes his head, no. The jingling sound again.

○

Younès never leaves a message. He calls, that's all. It becomes a routine: she sees Gabriel's face, and she doesn't pick up. It's never the right moment—during a consultation, in the metro, in the evening, with her husband and the bottle. But he calls often enough for her to notice when he doesn't call. Moreover, every time he calls, she says to herself: *I did a really stupid thing*. The sentence becomes her ringtone. Women often tell themselves they're stupid, and they're so often told that they're stupid, but this time, yes, she did a stupid thing by giving the phone to this stranger. She lets it ring as she stares at the old photo of her son's face, still round and a bit chubby. When her real son calls, a more recent photo appears, he's fifteen instead of fourteen, his blond hair cut short and now almost brown.

She is frightened he'll ask her to do things she won't be able to do. Promises. Money. Commitments she won't be able to keep. A bit of money would be okay. But more money? Or what else? Grichka she can handle. Grichka and his mother and the others. She has the expertise. She can go the distance. And there's the institution, structures, direction, evaluation, colleagues. Admittedly the institution has its problems, but when it comes to Younès she has nothing. She should contact an organisation. But all of those bleeding hearts with their simplistic views. He's calling to ask for something. For sure. Not to have a chat.

At the moment, Younès is somewhere. *At the moment*, she wonders. Where? What shape is he in? If he's calling it means he's not dead. Unless someone has stolen the phone from him. Younès. Becoming more and abstract. She tries to persuade herself that there is someone at the end of the line, the way one persuades oneself, by dint of reason and imagination, that right now there are galaxies above Paris and real whales in the sea. She's looked on Facebook, but apparently there are thousands of Younèses in the world. On MagicMum she learns that Younès is Arabic for Jonah. The third blue line of entries brought up by the search engine refers to a Younès Abaaoud, a 'caliphate lion cub', fifteen years old and just entered the ranks of Daesh. The lion cub has round cheeks and is trying to grow a beard. It's not her Younès.

One day he sends a text. A very formal text. 'The face of the Mum gives me strength and courage.' What does that mean? Is he *flirting* with her? Is he trying to seduce her in order to extort money from her? Or identity papers? She needs to calm down. 'The face of the Mum gives me strength and courage.' It's a bit mawkish. Or poetic? Like a mantra. I am a Mum. That is my identity. He is looking at me and I am protecting him. From now on, whenever he calls, she focuses hard on sending him good vibes. She tries to transform herself into one of those devotional images people hold in their hands when they need to pray. An icon. A Virgin Mary. Of course, in Niger they're mostly Muslim. After checking, she learns from her cheeky son that the photo he used for 'Mum' in his contacts is the one taken at Easter, when she was wearing a headband with rabbit ears that belonged to Emma.

She feels like an old white woman fantasising over a young black man. And she's trying to remember the young black man's face. His uneven forehead, his wet curly hair—she can see his eyes, his delicate hand. She can't visualise the rest; it's lost inside the ship with the drenched fabrics, the large Nigerian woman in Gabriel's sweater, the drips, the noise, and the sound of something stalling, rasping, like a seized-up motor. At night she dreams that she has trouble walking. She is moving down a corridor, but not forward. There's something both in her hips and in space, in her body and in the three dimensions. One foot. The other one. She loses her balance. It's like some sort of gum, like mounds of glue, something impassable that she can't see and that she steps over in horror.

For a while now she has found it more painful than before to distinguish interior from exterior. How to explain it? Is it the era (this new millennium) or that she's getting older (her age)? Her generation is on the brink of disaster while also being the most fortunate (especially women, when you compare with areas of the planet that are still uncivilised). She is certain that her premonitions of destruction trigger far greater feelings of anxiety than those experienced in the Dark Ages. Hence the importance of the house. Of being in a safe place. And better than in Paris. She'd like a Tupperware house. Hermetic, clean, durable.

In between patients she goes on Google Earth and looks at their house in the village. Its sturdy roof, its enclosed garden, its small pond, and all the other individual houses in the very green area of the residential estate, the perfection of the location, neither too close nor too far from the city, and the ocean fifty kilometres away: when she zooms out, she can see its huge blue rim. Her inheriting the house was not a complicated business: her parents and grandparents, rattled by History, reproduced sparingly, and the sale of the Paris apartment easily covers the inheritance tax and the renovation. That's how Rose became the owner of this family home of four bedrooms and convertible attics on a sizeable block, three thousand square metres, on the surface of the Earth, in a moderate climate, temperate and a bit windy, at the bottom of the Bay of Biscay.

As long as the Gulf Stream continues to flow. She zooms out again. The yellow waters of the Adour River pour into the blue sea; the dark blue further out indicates deep-water trenches, where amazing creatures perhaps still exist. She zooms in again. There's the tiled roof; she tries to spot herself there, to make out her own family through the slightly out-of-focus satellite image. Like a photo of the future. But the photo is old: her grandmother's Renault Scenic is still parked in front of the house. It's weird.

She's applied to work at the two local psychology clinics; she'd have a bit of a drive to get to the one on the coast, but it's a pretty trip. She hasn't said a word here about leaving.

Her next patient is late, so Rose crosses the

Atlantic. There are mountains beneath the sea and a very long fault line that makes a fontanelle in the ocean's skull. She arrives in New York, zooms in on Amityville, Long Island. A classic example of the unsellable house. Her husband is fascinated by it. The sextuple murder in 1974. And yet 'the house of the devil' was sold and resold. The retirees who were living in it when the famous film came out swear they never noticed anything abnormal. In a few clicks, Rose finds out that this 'stately' home with a pretty garden, five bedrooms and four bathrooms, on an inlet an hour from New York, is worth, more or less, a million dollars.

She raises her head and out her office window sees the bitumen terrace where the creche next door has set up a pitiful toboggan. And she thinks of days by the sea, in the future and in the past. In Clèves, yes, another life will be possible, in the greenness, in the blueness, in the sunshine.

'I'm going to break everything!' yells Bilal. He has waited five minutes too long in the waiting room, waiting is one of the things he doesn't know how to do, and getting him into her consulting room is always an adventure, transitions terrify him, thresholds, changeovers, *I'm going to break everything*. For the time being, Rose regards him entering her office as the treatment itself, therapy, care. Let him come in, accept to be invited in, and let him keep the weekly appointment. Each sentence he utters is progress, and if he says he's going to break everything, we can only hope he won't.

Right now Bilal is grabbing one of the consulting-room chairs.

'Bilal,' she says.

Bilal is screaming so loudly that no sound can reach him. The chair flies in the direction of the computer and Rose visualises Cervix smashed to pieces—but no, the chair bounces off the wall.

'Bilal,' repeats Rose. Her phone rings; she has forgotten to put it on silent. She reaches for her bag to turn off the noise, but Bilal is now furious, really furious. He twirls onto the couch with such a quick pirouette that wings seems to sprout from his back.

'Bilal!' she protests. She picks up the chair, but Bilal grabs it again, she holds one leg, he holds the other, this is not working, she lets go, this time he throws it very hard against the door, with maximum impact. He's right, everything has to be broken, but for now she's going to terminate the session. Getting

Bilal to leave is as difficult as getting him to come in. Bilal is trapped in her circle of ashes, just like in *Nosferatu the Vampyre*. She tries doing the same thing she saw in the movie: she rubs her feet against the linoleum and scatters imaginary ash. Dumbstruck, Bilal stops beating his wings. He is eleven years old and as tall as her. She bends over to blow on the ash, their heads brush against each other. They both look at what is blocking the way. They look at the invisible thing on the floor.

The spell is broken as soon as she opens the door—Bilal starts screaming again.

'You return him to me far more upset than he was!' his father remonstrates. He addresses the whole waiting room: 'Rose Goyenetche is *never* on time, none of this serves any purpose, and the centre used to be closer—'

'I know,' says Rose. 'They're shutting down the psychotherapy services in this area.'

Bilal screams.

'What I need,' says the father, 'is for you to help my son.'

They're in agreement. She offers him her hand. A tremor of fear runs through her: as long as he's not one of those men who don't want to shake hands with women. But he takes her hand and the fluid passes gently between them, the noise level lowers and she recovers that muted contact with the space around her, with the linoleum beneath her soles, and with the father's goodbye—a small amount of trust recovered too, between them, in her, in what she does.

Younès has left a message. His first voicemail. She has no idea why she doesn't listen to the message in her office. It's as if there was a better distribution of noise and silence downstairs. And yet there's construction work in the lobby. The director is having a diagnostic centre built, where each child will have a check-up. A team of workers, all black, are repainting the area in salmon pink. Their radio is blaring. Younès's message is almost inaudible; as happens with messages from some of her patients, she only catches one in three words. Fortunately she can listen to it as many times as she needs to: he hopes she's well, she and all her family and her children, by the grace of God, and then repeated syllables, *ga-day-lie-on*, what? Lions, the caliphate lion cub? *Gare de Lyon*, of course. He's arriving at Gare de Lyon. At 7.37 in the evening. He rolls his *r*s. He's coming. Today. This evening.

She stares at the lobby. The old embossed beige wallpaper is still visible wherever the salmon-pink paint hasn't yet been applied. There are still a lot of power points within reach of fidgety kids' fingers— you'd think it was a means of getting rid of them.

Like a net, an immense fatigue descends over Rose's shoulders. Cesária Évora is singing on the radio, then a man starts talking. He's talking about the migrants because everyone talks constantly about the migrants.

> *No more ifs or buts: a true narrative is emerging. It is not our mission in any way to be an undercover agent for political parties; if the proposals put forward by the extreme right resemble ours, that is your call and we duly take note of it. For example, we should consider what Georges Marchais, a leading light of the left, said back in 1980: that economic immigration was not desirable for France as its effects were detrimental to French workers. It is worth noting that, of the people in Calais, only one per cent are Syrian refugees and all the rest are Eritrean, Sudanese, Afghan. So they are not people who are fleeing from war. On the ground it is perfectly clear. I am viewing this situation with, yes, one could say, absolute certainty. We're familiar with the Syrian-refugee defence being used to bolster the other economic cases,*

and of course in between there are humanitarian cases that merit our attention. But this is not the key issue. Our aim as an association is to help local citizen collectives do battle on an equal playing field with the state and media powers that be, who are disseminating falsehoods.

She places her hand flat on the embossed wallpaper. Her husband often talks to her about feng shui, the Chinese philosophy of the built environment: we have to make peace with buildings, transmit energy to them through our offerings. The old hospital groans. She thinks she hears Bilal.

She changes at Gare du Nord for the high-speed RER, then runs. The babysitter leaves at 7.30 p.m. and her husband is never home before eight. Too bad, Gabriel will look after Emma. In most countries in the world they'd already be independent, right? She pushes against the crowd to get into the carriage; the doors shut behind her. She fixes her gaze in space with the same precision that she does her body. Do not make eye contact with anyone. Now that her flesh is no longer young, she is less vigilant about wandering hands, but over the last few years her skill at avoidance techniques has increased exponentially, out of fear that, amid the bodies, a hostile body actually might explode.

And it's only because she is so used to public transport that Rose can absent herself for a few minutes, drift in the space-time continuum, her eyes half-closed, hanging on to a strap. Beneath her eyelids, she can see Clèves; she follows a specific road, dashing along; she arrives at the bottom of the village and the river appears before her in a flash. It's summer, the blue of the sky and the green of the water; it's a particular spot upstream, the little weir where the salmon go through.

At Gare de Lyon there is the usual backwash of rushing commuters and anxious out-of-towners. She pushes like everyone else. It's 7.33 p.m.; she only has four minutes and it's the biggest train station in Paris. And he didn't tell her *where* he was coming from: Nice, Toulon, Marseille? She tries to spot the 7.37 on the arrivals board. She could call him—no. Why doesn't she call him? What is she going to do? Welcome him to Paris? They're moving house in four months. She visualises the house in Clèves. It's a large house. But anyway, that's not what he wants, what would he do in Clèves?

The sky is filled with interlacing pipes and black

concrete. Intersecting escalators carry their enormous cargo of passengers along a glass wall protecting a grove of palm trees. The passengers distribute themselves rapidly and methodically from one place to another. It's not ugly; it's efficient. She has the impression the station is going to fold itself over her like a giant envelope and post her somewhere—off you go!

The commanding female voice of the station's PA system announces the departures and arrivals. *Please stand back from the edge of the platform.* The train is here. 7.37. Come on, get a grip. The passengers descend on her, she tries to focus on individual faces, moves forward a bit, then, so she won't be jostled, she shifts sideways to a spot behind a large hanging sign: *Bomb alert. All luggage may be inspected.* An icy wind comes off the platforms. She buttons up her jacket, ties her scarf around her head. Wonders fleetingly what she's trying to hide—her rabbit ears? She's about to lean on the sign, but there's no backing. The platform is empty. She can't see him. Her phone rings. It's him. Behind the photo of Gabriel. She must change it. Just enter *Younès* in Contacts and be done with it.

It was a good thing that she gave him a phone. A phone is already a lot. Plus the plan that came with it—that's a commitment. They live in a fifty-eight-square-metre apartment. She looks at the phone vibrating in her hand. The dead bodies on the bridge and the brave captain flash before her eyes. We should be living in a brave country and on a brave planet that bravely distributes its occupants. She doesn't have the strength. She hasn't even spoken about it to her husband.

The platform has cleared and he is there, alone, his outline distinct, his head bowed, studying his phone. He lifts his head and looks around. Tall, thin, shorter hair and—it's heart-wrenching—wearing Gabriel's parka. He hasn't sold it or swapped it or lost it, or whatever. He's kept it. Because he needs it. And it's cold on this platform. Her courage fails her. She takes advantage of a last group of passengers to retreat.

She hides out at the Relay newsagency. Now it's pitiful and it's dragging on. He's still standing there, a transparent plastic bag twisted around his wrist. It's hard to make out what's inside, but it looks like a can of Oasis soft drink and a pair of large gloves. He has no other luggage. He's staring around, sort of swivelling. Apart from the cleaning crew, the platform is completely empty. He's on another call. But not to her.

He makes a move. At first it's barely perceptible. He fidgets. Then he heads off without hesitation, the phone to his ear. Now he looks like almost anyone else. She can't see him properly, just a glimpse at the end of the platform. The station opens up in front of him like a sea. She imagines her son in a foreign country, in front of all those faces, all those bodies, all those people going somewhere. In front of newsstands, ticket counters, queues, the chemist, cafes, staircases, neon lights, the police, the military police, security guards, homeless people, the Roma, the night lights outside, the city. He is still looking around. She lowers her head. What else should she do? Give him some money and make her escape? Pay for a hotel room for him? Or give him the key to the house in Clèves? Why is she hellbent on sending him to the country?

He heads towards Paris, the phone still against his ear. So he has someone else apart from her? Or is he trying to put on a brave front? The luminous little fluoro strips on Gabriel's parka zigzag through the crowd. She starts to follow at a distance. People bear down on her as she moves against the flow; it feels as if they are the only two heading in this direction, towards the huge spillway of the roads, at the top of the congested square, crowded with taxis, from where you can get a bit of an overview of Paris, the twelfth arrondissement, the sex shops and cafes, the bus stops, the metro station, the Vélib' rental bikes, the cars, the pedestrians, the dogs, the Parisian trees and this strange, steamy night.

She sees him, from behind, seeing Paris for the first time. It's a risk. He will either dive in or turn around to face her: enter the city or look behind. All she can see is the back of the parka, the sleeves with those fluoro bits, the thin legs in the thin pair of jeans, the plastic bag, the short hair. Faltering on the threshold. She hopes his eyes are shining. She hopes: shining with joy and adventure and youth. She prays: let his eyes shine with joy. Yes, she would like her powers to extend well beyond what she knows; she would like to be an incognito heroine in the city, and accompany him with her magic powers. She would like to surround him with a cosmic shield, so that, incombustible, he could sail through danger, laugh with joy, with Paris before him.

Paris. She hears the name as she did when she was a little girl. *Paris*, the enticement in the first syllable and the fresh air between her teeth, Paris, *partir*, leave. Leave her dump of a village and head up to Paris. He has come up from far away, following a meridian directly north from Niger. He crosses the crowded square. He turns left into the wide street. He seems to know where he's going. Or else he's doing a good job of pretending. She follows him. He is walking fast. As if he's been here before—the thought strikes her like a bolt of lightning—as if she's not at all witnessing his first contact with Paris. A little satellite touching down on the planet city. He looks at the Seine. It is black.

Now he's heading along the road by the river, the freeway that shoots cars towards Notre-Dame in the west and Bercy in the east. The morgue is in the middle, between the two destinations. It seems to have been built right on the river so the drowned bodies can be fished out. There are very few pedestrians and a huge pile of dead bodies in the cube of bricks stuck on the edge of the water. Rose hides behind a plane tree, like in the movies. She used to live here, not at the morgue of course, but opposite, at 70 Quai de la Rapée, when she first arrived in Paris. As a student. The neighbourhood used to be a building site. She walks along a past that has been entirely reconstructed. New buildings made of glass, on whose surfaces the student she used to be was never reflected, but who did, however, walk on this ground. She is now following a young unknown boy in a transformed space, a forty-something woman in a world of human migration.

He takes Charles-de-Gaulle Bridge, a new bridge, which she has never crossed on foot, and which looks like an aircraft carrier. The wind is blowing. A house-boat. Younès slows down, watching the long boat going past beneath him; she hopes he is feeling that childish joy of seeing that it only just gets through, that the pilot has manoeuvred perfectly. Now he's walking even faster than before, his head still bowed over his phone. He has pulled up the hood of the parka. Someone must be guiding him. Does he think the Seine is beautiful? Was he born on the banks of the Niger River? Is the difference between the two rivers unfathomable, or are they simply two rivers, each with its own waterway system, its own level and its own boats?

Rose and Younès are the only people walking on the bridge, along the pedestrian passageway. She hangs back, the whole length of the bridge between them. If he turns around he'll see her. But he's watching where he's going, towards the oppo-site bank. The Seine is narrow, four seagulls and a faint smell; she wonders if he's disappointed. What sort of view does he see? Is he looking for someone other than her, someone whose outline is more clearly defined?

At the end of the bridge he goes down a staircase; she trots along so she doesn't lose sight of him. She is dazzled by the green light from the City of Fashion and Design, right there, with its spectacular curved shape. Then her eyes become accustomed to the light and she sees, under the bridge, in the shadowy area near the first pillar, tens, hundreds of tents lined up, close together in three rows. She goes halfway down the staircase. She's lost him. The underside of the bridge resembles a wide, long Futurist ceiling, smooth, white, like a passenger boat run aground, and humanity has taken shelter beneath its hull. There are braziers and the outlines of figures.

Now she can see the people distinctly, standing, sitting, condensation on their breath beneath the pure lines of visionary architecture. She doesn't dare go any further. Everything is modern and outside of time, new and wretched, medieval and now. It is science fiction. Where is he? Has she betrayed him? She didn't say she would come. She didn't promise anything. She didn't reply. She thinks about how she is alone here, without telling anyone. She thinks about the vengeance of all these aggrieved men. Her body would be found in the river and she would be another Unknown Woman of the Seine. Her husband would go and identify her body at the morgue.

She climbs back up the staircase, along a ramp, then up another level. A man is coming down. The staircase stinks of piss and the guy looks at her and adrenaline surges through her heart: it's the guy from the cabin without portholes. The out-of-focus guy, who threw himself overboard during the cruise. He disappears into the night. She is going crazy. Or else the world is.

The ultra-civilised skyline of Paris opens onto the terrace bar of the City of Fashion. She has never been here before. Everything is young and hip and a bit intimidating. She is not dressed appropriately at all, but really, she'll be fine, a Parisian woman is naturally chic.

She just needs a glass in her hand. She opens her bag to show the security guards that she has neither weapons nor explosives and she sees the time on her phone: 8.23 p.m. There are several missed calls from her husband, and the real Gabriel is also getting worried via text: 'Where r u?' A babysitter who only stays until 7.30 p.m. is not enough, Rose has to be locatable the whole time.

She orders a mojito. With one gulp she is filled with warmth and good sense. That's better. She starts to think straight again. What came over her, to follow him into the city? Getting caught up in all this. It's not like her. Even going on a cruise is not like her. The only leeway she has in the world, her only course of action, the only thing possible for her, her *freedom*, for fuck's sake, is to make sure that children of all kinds do not fall victim to the general madness. It's her profession. There you have it. It is already a huge thing. It's her life.

A second mojito. The music is loud. The atmosphere is strange. Or else it's her—she no longer knows how to go out and have a good time. The crowd are all in their thirties, tall and elegant, mostly guys, wearing those beards they wear these days. Fashionable with the cool people and with the jihadists. Her son would tell her that it wasn't the same beard, and that no one says 'cool' anymore. Two of them to her left at the bar are kissing. Bearded guys. They're drinking Aperol spritzes. She should have ordered an Aperol spritz. Behind her a young woman and a young man are leaning on the railing overlooking the Seine and the tents two storeys below. The wind carries snatches of conversation her way.

'You do not build on quicksand, that's my motto. And José is quicksand.'

The girl, in high heels, wraps a magnificently coloured scarf around herself; the wind seems only to be there in order to offer her this dance, this grace, to fill her wings. Her boyfriend holds his glass out to her and smiles at her, he smiles at the girl and at the Seine, he even smiles at Rose. He seems to want to share his point of view: that life is beautiful, the world magical, and José quicksand.

'Gizmo means gizmo, something you discard. Otherwise, why say gizmo. I don't see why you'd go away for the weekend with someone you'd discard.'

The girl has an ironic smile, indifferent, she is drop-dead gorgeous. Why not grant them the same confusion that has her in its grip? The uneasiness that the poor people are below, and the rich are above? Whatever. It's nothing new. The little match girl died of hunger and cold beneath the windows of the banqueteers. For that matter, there is a small group of refugees, or whatever you call them, boat people, on the terrace a few metres below the revellers. It's ever so slightly porous between the two levels. The refugees are drinking their beers among themselves. Two security guards of the same colour keep watch. At five euros per beer, the surveillance is a doddle. She hesitates. She could go over to them and say his name. Younès. Ask. She orders an Aperol spritz. She rests her elbows on the railing, and she sees him. The fluoro strips. Gabriel's parka dances like script among the braziers. She stays there, leaning on the railing, hypnotised, her glass in her hand above the zigzagging little traveller.

III

'What is worse than being outside?
Outside with nothing.'

TOM-TOM
Caritas France, Calais

If she made a list of the reasons why they were compelled to leave Paris, on it would be—but in what order?—the impossibility of finding a decent home even with two salaries, the deterioration in her working conditions, his real-estate battle and the ghosts, the terrorist attacks, the elections, her unfulfilled appetite for gardening, their search for an outcome other than divorce, the strange problem of Emma's schoolbag, Gabriel's general aimlessness, their need for some fresh air. She's gone down the road as far as she can with Bilal, and with Grichka and his mother and the extraterrestrials. Even if she refers them to her best colleagues, she knows she'd be leaving them in the lurch here. And Younès. This has nothing to do with Younès. Anyway, she hasn't told a soul about Younès.

She is going on a last walk—not the last, no, she will come back, there's just the difficult, surreal notion of having to stay in a hotel or at friends' houses if she got the urge to *visit* Paris. She walks along a road by the river where painters and poets used to live. A blue sky floats over the city. The weeping willows are wearing their pale, gauzy leaves, the cobblestones are ancient, the weather is mild, the *bateaux-mouches* travel up and down the river, the tourists queue out the front of the ice-cream shops, she feels the warmth of the sun shining through little white clouds. Notre-Dame here and the Hôtel de Ville there. The Tour Saint-Jacques. The morgue in the distance behind the plane trees. Spring is on its way and it's already hot. Summer will be scorching. In the country, will she miss Paris? Most likely she'll miss her girlfriends and her Pilates class.

Emma's schoolbag reinforced, if that were necessary, their decision to leave. For a while now, even though they washed Emma, and changed her clothes, a smell lingered around her. A pungent, overpowering, disgusting smell—the smell of shit. Accompanied by a raging flare-up of her eczema, but they're used to that with Emma, they slather her in cream, restrict her to sponge baths—the water in

Paris is very hard, the ground beneath the city, the sewers and the catacombs is an immense limestone quarry. But the smell doesn't go away. Emma no longer wants to go to school, but as Emma has never wanted to go to school, they hustle her to get up, get dressed, swallow her Honey Pops and be obedient, and think of all the little girls who don't have the chance to go to school.

The babysitter complains about the smell. On the second or third night—the night of the Gare de Lyon escapade, to tell the truth—Rose decides to go and give Emma a kiss even if it's late, in her bedroom that is, admittedly, too small, but where Rose has always felt happy. Only now does she become fully aware of the permanent odour of shit, now that it dominates the familiar smell of onion and meat from the kebab stall below. Gabriel has emphatically decamped onto the living-room couch. Emma is not asleep. She is crying under the pink doona. Her eczema is so bad that Rose can barely make her out among the shades of bright pink. Her cheeks are as fuzzy as the fabric. Rose kisses her, she strokes her sweaty hair off her face, wipes her eyes, her nose, and then all her strength dissolves. She's failing to look after her own children.

She buries her head in her daughter's neck. She wants to console herself, find comfort in this little girl who is crying. She asks her questions about her day, about what has happened, but the child doesn't answer, she never answers. If she utters the odd word it's only to talk about animals: a dog that looked at her in the street, a whale at the bottom of the bathtub. She has never talked about what happened on the Acropolis, whatever time warp she slipped into— or with whom. Rose hugs her more tightly, Emma protests. As Rose shuts her eyes in the pink shadows, she feels the effect of the two or three, perhaps three or four, mojitos and Aperol spritzes she drank at the City of Fashion and Design. She has to protect Emma. Protect her. She understands what's going on with Grichka's mother and the helmet. She needs to invent a full-length deep-sea-diving outfit for Emma. Erect lightning rods around Emma, build sarcophagi as thick as the one around Chernobyl.

Where did she go wrong? When Emma was a baby, if an adult in her presence unthinkingly talked about some shocking event, Rose always rectified things immediately: 'The world is not like that, Emma.' She shouldn't have. She should have toughened her up, let her discover the degree to which the world could not care less about one more little human being.

She keeps cuddling her, despite the smell. The energy accumulates and rises in a dome shape above them. Her strength returns, and she feels capable once again of facing up to the outside world. And, in this minuscule bedroom, the outside world is the smell. The first sign of demonic forces in the Amityville house were the awful smells. Perhaps horrible things have happened here too? A child martyr. A hanging.

She gets up to unhook from its hanger a little coat that is casting a shadow. She trips on the straps of the schoolbag and bangs into the wall. Shit. The smell has spewed out like some evil thing. It's the schoolbag. The inside of the bag is slathered with shit. On the bottom is a squashed turd. Someone shat in Emma's schoolbag. The exercise books are stuck together with it, everything has to be chucked out. How long is it since this bag was opened? To think that we pay a babysitter to supervise her homework, and the child won't say a word. Who did this?

Rose is crying so loudly that Christian comes in and reels backwards when the stench hits him. 'We have to get her out of that school,' he yells. He's been saying it for months, and Emma is now crying her eyes out too, they have to get away from it all, leave it all behind.

She summoned Grichka and his mother to a meeting; she has something urgent to say to them. Here we are: she's had a brainwave, a flash of insight. 'As if I had received a message.' Grichka is silent, tense: he knows that Rose is speaking the language of mothers. 'Psychoanalysis,' says Rose, will take care of the electromagnetic waves.' She raises her hands to her temples. 'From now on I will be your receiver. Think of me as an earthly antenna or a lightning rod.' She spreads her hands in front of her. Her heart is pounding. Perhaps it's starting to work. But the mother wants her to provide further explanation.

'Daniel Schreber, the subject of an essay by Freud on paranoia, said that extraterrestrials—he called them "God"—had connected "divine rays" to his head.' Rose pulls her hair up in the air, miming. She can tell the mother is still sceptical. Rose perseveres: 'Thanks to this transferral, connections can be made without using any high-tech equipment or other expensive or cumbersome gear. Grichka can do it without the helmet.'

She places her hand on the mother's shoulder,

as a mother, as a teacher, as a sister, as whatever you want. She wills everything into her hand. She doesn't feel any immediate transmission, but there is a strong muscular relaxation nonetheless. Grichka gives her a grudging smile of admiration.

Nothing happens for a few seconds. But the mother, holding on to the armrests, her head back, looks like a cosmonaut at lift-off. Rose squints and waits for the big moment of ignition, take-off…That moment when the motors fire on all cylinders, when going back is no longer possible…She has a vision of herself on a road with her children, the apocalypse behind them, something like the smoking ruins of Paris razed to the ground. And she remembers a story from her grandmother, the one who left her the house in Clèves, along with her strength: she knocked on a door during the 1940 exodus and was refused a glass of water for her child. She can see and feel all that, snatches, flashes, capsules of time.

The mother wakes them up by saying, 'Okay.' Rose performs a final little conjuring trick, placing her hands above Grichka's helmet. There's a jingling sound even though she isn't touching it. Even though Grichka isn't moving. Good. She releases the straps under his chin and removes the helmet, careful not to pinch him. There is a tiny electrical pop when they brush against each other. Grichka giggles because it tickles him and because the skin on his skull can breathe again and his vision is clear now.

Time remains suspended for what seems like forever. But the extraterrestrials do not attack. The room does not begin to turn and there is no ringing sound. Grichka's mother manages to stay the course. Rose asks if she can keep the helmet, to run some tests on it. The mother acquiesces with dignity.

She tells Bilal that she is leaving and that he can break everything now. She has hidden the computer behind a little wall of books. But Bilal is dumbfounded. The departure of his shrink petrifies him. It's immensely disturbing to see Bilal motionless. He really should get moving again, but nothing happens. Stunned, he just keeps staring at Rose. Is there anything else you expect from your shrink, apart from being there?

Rose hesitates. She holds out her hand. The psychoanalyst and paediatrician Françoise Dolto never touched children who had not touched her of their own accord. But Rose gives herself permission, she would like to see if, with Bilal…the contact might…She places her hand on his hand. The kid remains stock-still. The fluid, if it is in fact a fluid, passes from her skin to his. It's very hot and almost painful. Bilal pulls his hand back, surprised. But it's as if they have had a proper goodbye.

She is really going to miss Bilal. So she can't help saying, 'Goodbye, Bilal—everything is going to be okay.' But the words sound like the trinkets on Grichka's helmet.

Now we're in the future. They have moved into the house in Clèves. It's for real now. Christian is the sales manager in the real-estate agency near the station in North B, fifteen kilometres from the village. Rose missed out on the only vacant position at the psychology clinic on the coast, but everything in its own time. Setting up the house comes first. The chief psychological problem here seems to be absenteeism due to the surf.

Gabriel has grown and is entitled to the biggest bedroom. Emma will be under the eaves in an attic room; it has its charm. Anyway, the yin and the yang have to be spread around equitably. From Los Angeles, Solange found them a feng-shui builder right here on the coast. His job is to harmonise the flow of energy in the structure. He put in windows where they never imagined there could be any. He changed the very direction of the house. He made them aware of blockages in the circulation of *chi*, especially when it came to her ancestors: the past must not weigh on the future. He didn't need to convince her.

Obviously none of this would have been possible in Paris, where the only margin for manoeuvre had been the position of the beds, and even then... Their feng-shui builder is a Spanish Basque guy whose clients also include Russian and English people. The coast, especially South B, has always been a cosmopolitan place; some of it rubs off on the village, even the backblocks.

The house is a construction site. It's a bit arduous to have left Paris for this. The polished concrete has not even been poured and the floor is a sort of trench, with wires and pipes and God knows what else—it looks like open-heart surgery. For the time being, they all have to sleep in one room. There's a mountain of boxes stacked up under the terrace awning—not a single wardrobe has been assembled yet.

The garden is a wilderness, but it has always been like that. Rose has plans: dig out the brambles and invasive plants to create something like a meadow, where sheep could perhaps graze. The good thing about this garden is the pond, which they need to clear so that migratory birds can perhaps nest there. During her last weeks in Paris she daydreamed about the pond and the spring that runs into it: in the event of a disaster they would have enough to drink and to make a vegetable garden. When Paris is burning, when Europe contracts into a fist, she daydreams, looking at the garden.

They are having a drink with Arnaud, one of Rose's old schoolfriends. Arnaud is filling them in on the news about Delphine, Lætitia and poor Monsieur Bihotz. They tell him the news about Solange. He had already heard it, of course—who doesn't get news about Solange, through the media or the internet. Rose recognises in Arnaud that hint of malice she wants to avoid in herself: envy. Even the disastrous politics complicating their friend's American dream gives them an ounce of pleasure. She, Christian and Arnaud discuss all this, not the complications of Solange's life, but the effects of all these elections on the world, even on Clèves. Arnaud thinks we need tough men. It's unbelievable how Arnaud has aged. He is thin, and his skin is wrinkled, red and shiny.

It's a Sunday in July. They're sitting on a wooden

beam facing the overgrown garden and the cement mixer. Rose tried looking for the champagne glasses, but it was impossible to find the right box. So she rinsed out the tumblers they'd been using since they arrived. In the kitchen the temporary hotplate was filthy and they were skirting around the Ikea furniture that had to be returned because it was the wrong size.

Rose feels a bit like crying. But it will pass.

When Arnaud arrived she went outside into the bright sunshine of the unfinished terrace and greeted him with a kiss—it's been a while—and they laughed because there was a crackle of static as their cheeks touched. Christian uncorked the champagne. Arnaud smokes a lot and drinks as much as Christian. Indeed, they finish the champagne and Christian goes to hunt around in the kitchen for a bottle of rosé. She drinks a beaker of lukewarm rosé and scoffs peanuts. She has just caught sight of her reflection in the new patio door and she's happy with what she sees, but she knows that in a mirror, a real mirror, her features would be blurry. As for the Pyrenees, they are clearly defined, close by in the south wind, which seems to be carrying the mountains all the way to the village.

The neighbours opposite sold off their garden and three small subdivisions sprang up, three small villas; now they've ended up all living on top of each other. Each cleared block is supposed to be replanted with three trees, but oaks take too long and they lose their leaves, so there's hardly any shade: they all agree that albizias, dwarf palm trees and bay laurels do not count as trees.

'But bay trees ward off bad luck,' says Arnaud. 'You should always plant a hedge of them around a house. Not necessarily bay laurels, ordinary bay trees are enough, the ones you use for seasoning, the ones from around here.'

Now Arnaud and Christian are talking about the local real-estate market. Holiday houses are starting to be worth more than principal residences. The best properties are inherited, sales are rare. On the other hand, there are a lot of shoddy buildings that have ruined the coast, set higgledy-piggledy on top of each other in the seventies. Arnaud used to be the deputy mayor in Clèves. After a dispute he brushes over (but who has not had a dispute with Arnaud at some point?), he walked away from everything in order to cultivate a gift he has: he became a shaman. In fact, in order to bless their house, he digs into his pockets and takes out a clove of garlic, a star anise, a sprig of chamomile and juniper—it drives away demons.

They take him on a tour. From an energy point of view, the layout of the rooms meets his approval. The cellar is the only place he shies away from: 'It's crowded in there,' he says. 'You should plant a lily in front of the door; it placates the souls of the dead.'

Once Rose sets up her consulting room, Arnaud continues, there could conceivably be a synergy between the two of them. The number of bewitchment cases in the region is on the rise, but Arnaud is not an exorcist and priests are no longer believers. Her husband is agreeing wholeheartedly; he's always said that she neglects the special power she has in her hands.

Rose thinks back to Grichka. She doesn't really want to drive away ghosts. Once again, she feels a bit like crying.

In the evening, when they have settled Emma and Gabriel on the same mattress in the same temporary bedroom where they will also sleep, they go outside. The children seem more or less happy. Gabriel spends all his time on his phone, but when they tell him off he says he's writing. Emma is simply relieved to have escaped the life she had. But their parents are in a state of panic. The new quotes from the builder, the furniture in storage units, the leaking terrace, the nursery owner who has all their plants ready but whom they have to keep waiting, and the electricity, which is not even connected in her consulting room. They decided to put off their dream of having a pool and this burst of financial common sense made them feel better at the same time as it depressed them. They're fucking RPP, says her husband, laughing: rich people's problems. But they are not rich, apart from having sold their apartment in Paris, on which there was still a mortgage, and it feels to Rose as if they are the last remaining members of the middle class before the collapse of their world.

Her husband is lurching but the night air soothes him. He can breathe easy again: the house is their bright future. A channel of white breaks open the sky: the Milky Way in July over the south of France, no clouds, no street lights, no cars. Her husband points out Sagittarius, Orion and the Lagoon Nebula. She feels vaguely elated. Perhaps it's because she's sipped rosé all day. In Paris, beneath the opaque sky, she could never see further than the following week.

'Perhaps there are thoughts up there,' says her husband. 'Perhaps there are other feelings, other ways of being in the world. Perhaps there is a solution.'

They walk side by side. She inhales big breaths of fresh air, as if dragging on a joint. She thinks back to Grichka again, of course. And she thinks about Younès—can he see the same stars?

When they met, her husband owned a telescope. He wanted to be an astronomer. All he ended up doing was a bit of astrology.

But tonight he's on a roll. 'We see the Milky Way from the side,' he explains. 'It's a huge spiral but as we are right on the edge, we see it as a ribbon.'

'Aren't we at the centre?' asks Rose, who has gone back to the innocent tone of her schoolgirl questions, when she admired this tall young metaphysical man.

'We are actually a long way out,' continues her husband. 'We're on a tiny planet on the periphery of the galaxy.'

Rose (perhaps it's the rosé) has an attack of claustrophobia, right there under the stars. Gravity holds her close to the Earth's crust and she has a vision of herself as a minuscule person in a minuscule village on a minuscule planet spinning around in the suburbs of the world. At least the extraterrestrials will have heard of Paris: who does not know its name? She hangs off her husband's arm, he's surprised, they both almost fall over in the middle of the road. Here's hoping the neighbours aren't looking. And he nods in the direction of their house, the only one still with lights on.

'Look at that white cube sitting at the end of the path. The potential of that basic, practical cube, refined over a long period of time, more efficient than caves and huts, waterproof enough for sleep not to be a problem. Just think,' her husband says, 'about how sleep immerses us in a state of such immense vulnerability that we have to be protected while we're in it. Every night we have to repeat the same thing: we retire without having to ask ourselves where or how. Something as regular as hunger. The mighty vampire himself has to take refuge in his crypt at every rotation of the Earth. We humans need to have a bed and a door that shuts. A dwelling. An address on the planet.'

Is now the moment to talk to him about Younès, what she should do about Younès?

'Don't think about how inconvenient moving house is,' her husband continues. 'Think instead that what is strange about a bed and a door that shuts is how fundamental the system is, how commonplace, even while it allows us to experience what is most private in ourselves, our dreams, our nakedness, our sexuality. To be there alone or not, asleep or awake, in the throes of a nightmare, brooding, escaping perhaps—but in a safe place.'

Sometimes her husband is sublime when he's drunk. She will talk about Younès with him later. She has the weird feeling of hiding a lover from him. Their steps on the path make a muffled sound in the milky night; the silence is barely disturbed by the distant four-lane highway and the rustle of the poplar trees close by. It is so silent that, as they approach the cube where their children are sleeping, they hear the clinking of the spring water in the old pipe laid by her grandfather.

It's midday, in September, and she is drinking her coffee; her nails are black with dirt after weeding. It's midday and she is looking at the garden through the patio door. She is going to unpack still more boxes, it's coming to an end, she is coming out of the predictable chaos of moving in, all summer spent building shelves. Then she'll go and pick up Emma from school, from the new school where this young life is regenerating. Gabriel comes home on the school bus, which is a novelty for a Parisian, and nothing would indicate that he is thrilled by the experience.

She turns the radio back on. She had no memory of the silence here. Nothing happens. Not a single car, no passers-by on the path. The plants grow. The growth rings on the trees increase. The oak tree is starting to lose its acorns. *Plop* onto the terrace. She sweeps. A small tourist plane flies over the housing estate like a dragonfly. *Vrrrr.* It heads off towards the Pyrenees, over there, in the contrail.

Her phone vibrates and, before she even looks at it, before she even sees Gabriel's name come up, she knows it's Younès. She still hasn't edited the contact details. It's odd, she wants to talk to him, tell him about the move, the countryside, this big change of life. She watches the phone vibrating like a giant insect on the table. Storms are being forecast on the radio, a warning for the south-west; she'll have to close the shutters.

The silence sets in again. She has left her business card at the medical centres, the physios, with nursing staff, in chemists. The village GP was happy enough to talk to her, but people here are with it: they're after coaching, personal development, nutrition or mindfulness. In the morning there's the school bus going past, and there's birdsong, and the neighbours heading off for work; at eleven the postman. But by two in the afternoon she doesn't know what to do with herself. It's the sound of nothingness. A round trip to the beach would take too long; Emma finishes school at four-thirty. Over summer Gabriel often complained that they didn't go to the beach enough. But what with the work on the house, the fit-out of her consulting room, the peak real-estate period for her husband...And now it's back to school. The last of the boxes. Here are the champagne glasses. In a box of breakables. She contemplates the stash of concave, shiny goblets. She wants to shut the box and jump on top of it with both feet. But she takes the glasses out one by one, wipes them and puts them away in the new cupboards, along with the big crystal vase that held their white wedding bouquet, and then all the other vases they've accumulated, the presents, the bric-a-brac, the impulse buys, and these soup tureens from her grandmother, and these sauce boats, these butter dishes, these little milk jugs. They will stay in the cupboard and be found after her death. Her ashes will be placed in a new vase bought especially for that purpose.

She tries to pluck up the courage to go down into the cellar. The other day she thought she heard someone whispering. Her heart leapt into her mouth when she encountered a crazed toad. And that dreadful box, full of baby clothes, Emma and Gabriel's little tops she has never been able to decide whether to throw away or give away...

It's sunny. Superb autumn weather, a powdery yellow light and leaves that are still bright green. Intensified by the wind from the south, the world stands out against the flat backdrop of the sky. The phone never rings. The Parisians are carrying on with their lives. Perhaps they're resentful: she's jumped ship, left behind the pollution, and even the Cervix software program. Before getting in her car, she wipes a rag over the windscreen, something she would never do in Paris. The rag comes away ochre-coloured. Her grandmother used to say it was sand from the Sahara. The landscape was becoming exotic, nomadic and scorching. She felt the urge to leave. But that's it for departures—they have left. It's done. They have arrived.

She buys some bread, some cheese and some wine at the Vival supermarket and calculates her travel time on the GPS so she can go to the fruit-and-vegetable depot before the school pick-up.

It's incredible how cheap the greengrocers are here. She decides to leave the village by the North B side. She drives along in the family hybrid they've leased. They have to have two cars; her husband has invested in a little electric vehicle. And right at that moment she realises that she's waiting.

Of course, she's been waiting all day. But at that moment she's waiting for a feeling that isn't coming. There was a forest here before, just past the local blacksmith's forge. But now there's a GiFi home-decoration discount store and a Husqvarna outlet and a Renault service centre, and a roundabout, and advertising hoardings, and another roundabout, and here's the fruit-and-vegetable depot. A bit further on and it's already North B. She was expecting trees, but there aren't any here these days.

She parks in front of the depot. And who should she see unloading crates of discounted plums but Raphaël Bidegarray. A floating fragment of the past, alive, standing there. Very tall. So he must have grown since high school. 'Gawd!' he exclaims. His *a* is very broad. 'Look who's back.' He puts down the crate, stands up. She holds herself straight. His tanned skin is no longer marked by acne, but is wrinkled, which suits him. He pulls out a packet of Fortuna cigarettes from the pocket of his overalls and offers her one. It's terrible: he smells of the same cheap perfume he used to wear back in the day, and she could, there and then, bury herself in his neck, his armpit, his chest, but she holds her breath so she can remain motionless, nothing happening but these whiffs of time.

The hot wind envelops them and sets the cables of the advertising flagpole flapping. Raphaël lights their cigarettes like an expert. She inhales, it's disgusting. She smiles at him. He says, 'So you're back.' The *r*s rasp as they did when they were young, that accent she forced herself to lose and which makes her born-and-bred Parisian children laugh. They chat for a while. And she thinks how right she was to leave Clèves, to choose Christian rather than Raphaël.

On the way back, she makes a mistake and takes the road towards home instead of the four-lane highway towards the school. She does a U-turn at one of the innumerable roundabouts. Except it's blocked in the other direction. What on earth was she thinking giving Raphaël her mobile number? They only had sex four times, and not even properly, back in that distant time before the internet, before the whole planet was asking, as in the Bill Clinton business, whether a blowjob counted as having sex.

Why was she being punished with a traffic jam on a Tuesday in the provinces at ten past four in the afternoon? Because twenty years of life, through some sort of shunting process, had emerged suggesting another possible outcome? The doors of the fruit-and-vegetable depot had kept opening and shutting, they'd been standing in the exact line of the sensors. And she had glimpsed, between the two doors, what seemed to be a road lined with trees, winding up and around Clèves in a spiralling roundabout, the crest of which, hidden in a white light, looked at worst like an enormous neon light, at best a gigantic orgasm, she thought as she changed into second gear, then immediately changed down. Nothing was moving.

There has been an earthquake in Papua New Guinea. A Russian dissident has been assassinated in Stockholm. The urban infrastructure is becoming increasingly multimodal; the mini electric car is already obsolete. She switches frequencies, Basque rock bands and Spanish radio stations; she can't find FIP, her favourite French music station.

She arrives late at the school. The principal tells her to turn left at the Xurumuxu windmill and to drive back up behind the Decathlon sports store; at this time of day, it's the smoothest run. They're still waiting for the first tram-bus line, due to start in two years, but there will only be one stop in Clèves, right at the end of the village, so she'll still have to drive anyway.

There's been an explosion on the RER B, over a hundred dead and the number is rising, peak hour, it's not yet known if it was suicide bombers or parcel bombs. Emma is complaining that her hot chocolate is too hot. Rose reprimands her so she can keep listening, and then, no, she turns off the radio so the child can't hear.

Her phone has grafted itself onto her hand, Gabriel is bent over his, he's also old enough for names to mean something: the names of those who could have been on the RER B between Bourg-la-Reine and Antony on this late afternoon. The first name that came to her mind was that of her husband. He often worked in that vibrant area, with its constantly mobile middle class—she called him to hear his voice, to know that he was alive, alive like Emma and Gabriel. He's in South B in a villa with a view. Yes, he'd heard the news.

'It's lucky we moved,' he says.

No. She wants to be back there. She wants to be in Paris. She scrolls down the news feed on her phone. She thinks of Bilal's father, who made the long trip on the RER B and who was always on time. She tries to remember people's addresses, if they had any connection to this train line. Of course it will happen again outside the capital, not in Clèves on their little train track, but it's bound to happen again outside the capital. Today, however, once again, it's Paris. Paris, her beating heart. Paris, the city that made her a Parisienne. She decides to send a text to Bilal's father. So she asks after the boy as well. Paris, loved, loving, wounded. Abandoned, betrayed: she should be there, to help, to give blood, to offer her services in a combat team of shrinks.

'Mum,' says Emma, 'my hot chocolate is too hot.'

At the sink, she runs cold water over her burning cheeks. The evening is unfolding like a terrorist-attack evening. She feels far away, very far away from the Bay of Biscay. She spends the next day paralysed, on Facebook and on a twenty-four-hour-news TV station that is screening over and over the same three or four images: a train ripped apart, a body under an emergency blanket, heroic police and a woman passer-by saying wise things. She tidies up, cleans her damn villa—she should have been doing her work, listening, looking after the bereaved, fixing what could be fixed.

Through the trees, which have grown a lot, Rose glimpses the house owned by Solange's parents. When they were little, they used to build dams in the stream; when they were older they preferred staying in her father's study typing stuff on the videotex terminal, Minitel. And for the first time, Rose, whose only nostalgic attribute is her slightly old-fashioned name, wonders if things might not have been better before.

She calls in to the community library. At this time of day there are only a few retirees and housewives, and Nathalie the volunteer, a friend from high school. People here have changed. They're more articulate, less rustic. Their clothes, their cars. She's having trouble adapting, integrating, even though she was born here. Take Nathalie, for example: after a physio course in Bordeaux she's back in the village, chic, thin, sporty, amazing holidays, Vietnam, Laos, Malaysia, and a few hours facilitating cultural activities for the elderly. The elderly, also chic and sporty, tend to talk only about local issues, but with a good deal of compassion for Parisians: the terrorist attacks, the stress, the metro.

Rose marvels that they still say *the village* when the place has at least three thousand inhabitants and there are no longer any cows or corn. And she's given up explaining that, actually, she misses the metro, its efficiency, its speed. And the city's extraordinary mix of people. 'Where are the black people?' Emma had asked. 'Will they come back here, to the village?' Will the world return to normal?

Slanting sunlight comes in through the bay window onto the shelves. Rose has got that thing in her chest, that emptiness, almost panic. She'd like to take an interest in Nathalie's community project, she'd like to stick her fingers in the Clèves power point and feel she belongs here. But all she can summon up, and oh how powerfully, is that elemental feeling from her childhood: she has to leave. She has to leave the village and let herself be swept up by the world. Far from here.

For now, she has to pick Emma up from school. The weather is something out of science fiction. The start of winter is so hot it could be the end of summer, if it weren't for some red leaves stuck on the trees as if they'd been irradiated. She found a part-time job at the psychology clinic in West C, two mornings a week and hardly worth the two-hour commute. It's 4.11 p.m. Her phone rings on the passenger seat; she reaches across, even though she's driving. Perhaps there's a problem with Gabriel's school bus? It's Younès.

She says, 'Yes, yes.' The same way she'd speak to her son. Patiently. She wants to throw the phone out the window, she's so stupid, but she says, 'Yes, yes.' She wants to apologise for her behaviour at Gare de Lyon, but what would she say to him, and he doesn't give her a chance. She pulls over so she can hear him better, she says, 'Wait, wait.' He's speaking fast, rolling his *r*s—she'd forgotten. It's him, him in an emergency, a concentrated version of him. He speaks and she listens, she barely understands but it's as if they've known each other for a long time, since the room on the boat, water dripping from the roof, the survivors under emergency blankets, and the dead bodies. He's talking about legs. He says he fell over. Then the line cuts out, and when the phone rings again it's on video, she's not used to it. He shows her his ankles, both terribly swollen. Behind him on the screen it's raining, he's only half-sheltering under a tarpaulin, Gabriel's parka is soaking.

'Where are you? Where are you?' she asks. He says a very long name that she doesn't grasp at all. She just guesses. 'Calais?' A figure leans into the screen, an older man who says the name again, a diabolical name, worse than Goyenetche. *Thetotlstationinthandustrialzon*, he repeats. Now she understands, the Total petrol station in the industrial zone. In Calais. They tell her how to find them, she rummages in her bag for a pencil and paper because she doesn't know how to take notes on her phone when she's on a call. Both of them are talking at the same time now. She raises her hand, stop, stop.

Younès has shut his eyes as if he needs a break from speaking and from the pain. She asks him if he's been to hospital. Younès. He opens his eyes and tells her he's tired, that he broke his arm earlier, and now it's his legs, it's not good. She understands. This boy is falling apart. He says something else. She says, 'Don't move,' as if he were going to escape. This is all going crazy. She's on her way. She's coming, she's on her way, she's coming to get him, make sure he keeps his phone on him.

She starts the car again. She remembers to breathe. She has the urge to get going straightaway, but first she's going to pick Emma up from school, prepare a meal, let her husband know, cancel the only patient she has tomorrow, and then set off at dawn. She's having a sort of recurring flashback of what just happened. Over and over again she sees the little luminous screen with Younès's face and the other man, framed in the rain, their three-headed conversation: all inside her car. We are already well into this third millennium that used to be the stuff of her dreams as a child. But in no dream, not one, was she speaking with a boy the same age as her son, emigrated from Niger, wounded in a makeshift camp, on a portable screen that doubled as a phone, inside a hybrid car.

She checks the weather forecast for the north of France; it's fifteen degrees cooler. She grabs some sweaters, her warm jacket, some old clothes of Gabriel's, and pulls on her skinny jeans, the ones she used to called her battle dress in Paris, the ones she wore that night on the cruise—except they've shrunk. No. What the hell. She's put on weight. It's because she no longer walks anywhere. They're in the country but always in the car—she absolutely has to lose weight if she ever wants to set foot in Paris again.

She does a satellite search for the Total petrol station in the industrial estate of Calais: it's two roundabouts after the highway at the end of Avenue du Commandant Cousteau. She types in 'Calais Jungle' and reads a few articles. What used to be the biggest shantytown in Europe is now, seen from above, nothing more than a yellow and green rectangle: sandy fields bordered by a housing estate, a farm, factories, a gravel yard, an equestrian club, a German anti-air-raid battery. The sea is there, the ferries are there, the entrance to the Tunnel under the Channel is there. She zooms out, England is there, incredibly close. Thirty-four kilometres. Geography is the only way to understand it.

She zooms out further, the edge of the Earth expands, green, blue, white, clouds over Gibraltar, yellow, the Sahara, and there is Niger. The trip from Niamey to Calais is along a perfectly vertical line—a meridian—'6000 kilometres, 87 hours by car', that seems optimistic, or '974 hours by foot'. 'This trip includes a ferry crossing. This itinerary contains tolls. This itinerary contains private roads or restricted access areas. This itinerary crosses several countries. Your destination is in a different time zone.'

The walking route goes from oasis to oasis. Then

the dotted line peters out. It's funny. No, it's not funny. She zooms in on the strip of water between France and England. She can see the checkpoints and speculates on how many different kinds there are: for heat-based human detection, trackable carbon dioxide, and mirrors on and under the trucks. On the screen, the trucks look like Lego pieces. Using Street View she can see the aforementioned migrants, in hooded windbreakers, blurry but quite unmistakeable along the roads of the industrial district, standing, sitting, walking, and she can see the cops as well.

She learns from Wikipedia that in Neolithic times in Pas-de-Calais everything took place on foot. The sea levels were very low. She also reads about the land, later named Doggerland, that surfaced and connected England to the continent. Trawlers have dredged the bones of huge land mammals, mammoths and cave lions from the depths of the sea. There is a submerged forest off the coast of Norfolk. She imagines the trees at the bottom of the water. Their ancient trunks. Travellers in diving suits, shod in lead shoes and crowned with oxygen masks, walk in the forest.

○

Her husband is onto his second bottle, repeating the words *in a legal way*. He was citing all the stories of people who help, and who are perhaps people-smugglers, or—he raises his glass in a conciliatory gesture—who pass themselves off as people-smugglers. Has she even calculated the risk of getting a Nigerian across France without ID papers? A Nigerien, she corrected him. *Rian* or *rien*, whatever, did she expect him to travel in the boot the whole way? But I won't be crossing any borders. She was pleading. You have to do things in a legal way, said her husband. In the end she heard *inalegal*, she was happy to become *inalegal* if that would help Younès, and repair, yes, repair his young body that has fallen apart, and repair the past too, everything that has happened to him. She doesn't want to tell her husband about her debacle at the Gare de Lyon, or the unanswered phone calls.

He finishes off the second bottle, talking about Gabriel and Emma, and then: 'And, what, so we'll put him in school here? You're going to drive across the whole of France for this guy?' She heads off agreeably to get him a third bottle of wine. All of a sudden he's asleep. She has to go to sleep too, so she can drive tomorrow.

The house is spinning around her, the renovations

finished. It spins slowly in the empty night, along with the darker mass of the trees. If only an unknown spacecraft would land, with flashing lights and strange sounds, or in a majestic silence, it doesn't matter, just an event of some kind…She looks at her husband, out cold, his insomnia masked by alcohol. When she was twenty, she would not have put up with it. Nor when she was thirty. When she was forty, she wanted to leave it all behind her; now she is forty-five and she has left Paris and this is her life.

Sometimes she finds him asleep on the toilet. She finishes undressing him and puts him to bed. Sometimes he half wakes up and lies on top of her, and a sort of minimal contact is established in the conjugal night. Out of kindness she lets it happen, and perhaps for him too, it's a matter of kindness.

To get from Clèves to Calais she takes the D112 to Viodos-Abense-de-Bas, then leaves the D11 and heads towards Rivière-Saas-et-Gourby. At the roundabout she continues straight ahead on the D33. She has chosen a man's voice to be her GPS guide; it seems to reassure her. The road runs along by the river, passes Arrast-Larrebieu and Guinarthe-Parenties. The landscape passes like a pixelated map. She follows the directions step by step, for fear of getting lost so early and so far from her destination; at the roundabouts before Dax she heads towards West C and finally hits the freeway; things are easier on the freeway. It's daybreak. She turns on cruise control and turns off the GPS and looks at the countryside and turns on Blondie. It reminds her of a time when things were simple. *Call me, I'll arrive, you can call me any day or night*, she bangs the steering wheel in time. She tries to think about what she's doing.

After Onesse-Laharie the whole forest is destroyed. It's an immense field of felled trees. A bit of heather and a lot of dead wood. Apparently the area was overrun by woodboring beetles, total necrophages. Young pine trees have been laid low by the hurricane. The third thunderstorm finished off the destruction wreaked by the first two. The horizon is everywhere. It looks like tundra. Further on, there are enormous fields of corn, and those big skeletal sprinklers, like dinosaurs with their coils unfolded. Light rain.

The freeway went past a secluded hotel, a sort of health resort in the forest, but with trucks out the front—perhaps a brothel. As for the windscreen wipers, Rose couldn't decide between the slow and the intermediate speed. She listened to France Inter, and slowed down at the triangular signs notifying drivers about the presence of deer. So there were still deer.

She was coming up to Bordeaux, to the smell: the paper-pulp factory was still operating, all that wood. Fences started to appear; small, low houses in gardens. And washing hung out in the rain. Rose felt for the woman (man?) who had left the laundry out in the storm. Felt for those who functioned in odd ways, who found it difficult to comply with reality, and who persevered. Come on, get a grip. France Inter's obstinately hail-fellow-well-met tone was infecting her mind. Her hybrid car would make the distance on a single tank. She had water and buck-wheat biscuits.

On the Pont d'Aquitaine she felt as if she was falling into the sky. The bridge climbed, climbed… and the car slid into greyness. She stopped in a rest area after Beauvoir-sur-Niort. She called her husband. Messagebank. She shut her eyes and, for a few minutes, went off into a world in which she had no children. Her fantasy was animated and compli-cated, her plans constantly thwarted, her projects ridiculed, there were pitfalls and prizes, and on her heels something so worrying that she did not dare look back. She advanced from one level to the next, like in a video game in which she was the participant, not the player. The children reconstituted themselves into a single child that weighed heavily in her arms and that she had not been able to feed for a long time. Her movements became slower and slower, she could scarcely lift her feet, the ground was soft and treacherous, every step weighed tonnes.

When she opened her eyes, the rest area reappeared before her as an incredibly safe place. She had been asleep for a good hour. She undid her seatbelt, threw the cardboard packaging from the buckwheat biscuits in the recycling. The freeway radio notifications were broadcast in the toilets. No incidents, no hold-ups, the route was clear.

Cruise control on exactly 127 kilometres an hour, GPS off, light not too bright, dry road surface, vineyards as scenery, only a few trucks, which she passed after anticipating in plenty of time, as fluid as a fish, crash barriers, ribbon of white lines—after Azay-le-Brûlé there's the sign for the town of Soudan, funnily enough there's no sign for Niger or Chad, or Nigeria. After Sainte-Catherine-de-Fierbois came Montbazon.

Later on, she arrived at Tours and crossed a bridge over the Loire. The sandbanks in the river were like inside-out oases. She had a fleeting thought that she would take Younès on a tour of the chateaus, no, first she had to make sure he got better. She made a mental tally of the rivers she had seen in person: the Ardour, of course, the Garonne (with the Gironde, does that make three?), the Seine, obviously, and yes, the Rhone, the Rhine, she didn't think so. The Thames on a school trip. She searched for other memories to sort through and count. Her mind wandered. At the end of the freeway a pool of shadow was growing larger. A mirage. Come on, get a grip. Counting her lovers didn't take long. Solange could make long lists of her lovers, but she couldn't.

Is there a river in Los Angeles? What time is it in Los Angeles? She had a vague inclination to call Solange, to tell her—what? That she was going to collect an injured kid, about whom she knew nothing, from under a tarpaulin in Calais? Solange would be completely carried away, imagining it was a love story, interracial what's more, or she'd dream up a glamorous adoption à la Angelina Jolie.

Where was the turn-off? She was heading in the direction of Chartres–Paris instead of Mans–Rouen. Damn. It was the same distance. Despite being tired, she felt up for it. Her aim was clear. Her life was a side issue, tracking alongside her. She had another little rest at Beauce. The freeway was slicing through cultivated fields. Everything was huge, empty and flat, the capital city over there seemed to be suctioning up her world, and here we are now, beneath the familiar reddish sky, the first low-rise buildings of the outer suburbs, and soon the supreme centre: Paris. The Eiffel Tower and the Montparnasse Tower and the Pantheon and the Butte Montmartre—the four cardinal points of her geography were intact. So Paris existed without her. Paris was there.

It was 4.16 and the traffic was not bad. Do not return like the horse to the stable. Do not go home. Head north. She entered a tunnel. A huge wave of affection—nostalgia must be the name for it—rolled over her like a bus. Affection for the city and for herself within the city, a kind of osmosis, yes: being small and over-adjusted to the big, easygoing city, knowing how to accommodate her little body inside the big body.

And as she continued from the Porte de Vitry to

the Porte de Bercy, the Porte de Vincennes, the Porte de Montreuil, from threshold to threshold, she made a never-ending departure from Paris. She pictured herself back there, here, at home, in the house— Parisians say house for apartment—racing down the stairs two at a time because the lift didn't arrive, throwing the recycling in the yellow bin, jumping over the gutter, saying hello to the Sri Lankan street hawker who has been there for years, crossing outside the zebra marks to run to the bus, reading the newspaper on her phone between the shopping trolley of a granny with mauve hair and the stroller of a young woman wearing a boubou, heading at the slow speed of the bus towards her patients, towards Grichka and Bilal and the others. But she was in her car with the Pyrénées-Atlantiques numberplate, 64, and a piece of her had remained here in Paris. Even if she wanted to come back, pick up her life where she'd left it, strangers were now living in the apartment in which she was now a ghost.

It was evening in the industrial zone of Calais. The Picardy region had been reduced to the windscreen wipers' dark semicircle, shattered by the glare from oncoming headlights. After a wrong turn at a roundabout, she followed the GPS directions down the long rue Yervant Toumaniantz, then came across more roundabouts in a semi-abandoned bit of terrain from which emerged cranes, silos, sheds, trucks, police vans and metal gates: a lot of metal gates, stark white under extremely bright streetlights. All of a sudden it was no longer the road that was lit up but the surrounding area, the fields or vacant lots on the other side of the gates.

She slowed down, crawling along. The landscape became incomprehensible. The space on all sides was carved up by the stark white gates, one row, another one, a third row, a fourth, as if the gates were guarding other gates and were only there to impound more gates, some high, some on a lean, or straight, some topped with rings of barbed wire, others not; from a distance it looked like weaving on a frame loom, drawings, patterns, bouquets of fabric flowers, a new range of Calais lace.

Younès stood out in front, glaringly visible. But it wasn't him. He was walking. He remained still, whether seated or standing. He was sheltering under walkways along with other Younèses. He was wearing a windbreaker, hood up, hunched against the cold. He was young and thin. At a roundabout under lights, he was kicking a ball, dribbling, shooting for goal, running after the ball, his breath coming fast in puffs of vapour. A truck stopped abruptly, Younès in its headlights.

The illuminated Total sign was a sort of French flag in a spiral—blue, white, red—and also orange, she noticed, how long has it been orange? The Total petrol station at the exit of her village used to be blue, white, red, like the first Carrefour supermarket that opened there—whatever, their meeting spot is under the Total sign. The petrol station also contains a La Croissanterie cafe—the sign is the outline of a pin-up girl holding a steaming cup of coffee that seems to be an extension of her arm. She's white on an orange background. The night is certainly well illuminated. She parks; hers is the only car. She sends a text: *I'm here*. On reflection, she sends a second text: *I'm in a hybrid, 64 numberplate, small Basque sticker. Green red and white*, she adds. She also sends a text to her husband: *everything ok*.

Hers is the only car, given that all the other vehicles are police vans and trucks. Three panel vans: one parked in plain sight not far from her car. Is that a problem? And two others parked further away in the shadows. The trucks, a good fifty of them, are parked in diagonal rows, filling all the parking places, including the few spots designated for cars. Not a single truck driver to be seen. It's odd; perhaps they're lying down in their cabins? There are a few people at La Croissanterie. Some of the truck trailers are open, the double doors gaping. The insides are empty, geometrical, black.

Rose keeps an eye out through the car window, and also checks her phone. Time ticks away. The satellite image she's zooming in and out of is probably already out of date because there are fewer gates— narrow white lines on the screen—than there are now. They seem to be growing out of a system of roots germinating in the tunnel, over there, and sending out shoots all the way to the port where the ferries dock. Their network joins up at the Total petrol station, which is meaningless except when you realise that the Total petrol station is, in actual fact, the last entry point into England: the gap, the last open area, the last accessible piece of ground, call it a public space, where trucks wait it out on the border. And the sea is there, invisible, hidden by the dunes. The sea to be crossed, the sea to be drunk. The little Total petrol station in the Calais industrial zone is thus one of the most well-guarded spots on the planet, as if it was this place they wanted to protect from an invasion.

Younès was smoking under the awning of La Croissanterie. Definitely not Younès: this guy was squatter and a bit older. He crushed his cigarette in the freestanding ashtray provided and walked swiftly to the toilets. A policeman, rigged out like Robocop, held the door open for him, before walking, at an identically swift pace, back to a blue, white and red panel van parked a few metres away.

Then something incomprehensible happened. There was movement, a shifting. A group of hooded figures emerged from the shadows, about thirty metres from the cops. Out of the bushes at the edge of the station. Moving slowly at first, remaining as long as possible in the shroud of darkness, then, like quicksilver, they broke loose and began to run. The cops began to run too. The two groups came together behind the trucks. Barely a sound. Then gasps. Rapid footsteps. The sound of metal blows. Fabric rustling. The boxy shadows of the cops standing out clearly from the shadows of the stealthy figures. Muffled shots, panting, running, then silence again.

What the hell was Younès up to, her Younès?

She made a concerted effort to see, to penetrate the night like a cat. Long conical shadows fell between the streetlights. Between the trucks the night also hollowed out deep trenches, all parallel and of equal thickness. It was like the negative image of other trucks, each one neatly lined up, the dark matter of terrestrial transport.

And then it all started up again. Towards the back of the car park people had gathered behind a semitrailer, and were trafficking who knows what at the door—so that's what it was, the trucks with the wide-open doors, a message: try somewhere else, I've come from England, I've finished, I am empty, I'm leaving in the other direction. The shadows bustled around a closed door, the caped shadows of the cops hurtled down on them, high-speed chase, cat and mouse, cowboys and Indians, back into the bushes. The images that came to her mind were puerile, but everything was puerile here, without the magic of children's games. At the border, however, *click-click* sounds were for real. All night long, obliviously, the border produced them. The sound of padlocks was the sound of the border.

Rose watched from behind her windscreen. The Total petrol station thrummed in this impossible landscape like another International Space Station. She was its rough draft or its final product. She was going to take off. Leave this absurd place. Or else transform into a secret passage, a fault line, a telluric vortex, sinking deeper and deeper into the Earth or into the sky.

Another small group of figures had got moving, and the cops were obstructing them. The back and forth continued. She looked at her phone. 7.19 p.m. A message from her husband: 'Be careful. I love you.' What if Younès didn't reply? What if he never turned up? How would she find him in this chaos? She should go and have dinner somewhere and go to sleep. She was tired. She could shout herself a room in a hotel and stay for a bit—in central Calais, where Rodin's *Burghers* were. She'd check out the sights. The Museum of Lace and Fashion. She'd eat oysters sitting opposite the sea she has never seen, the North Sea. She would forget all this. There are women who disappear. It's even quite common. The women leave everything behind, from one day to the next; a car and a cash withdrawal and they slip into another life, in hotels by the sea.

The cop from earlier, the one who had courteously held open the toilet door, was staring at her. There was nothing to do but fill up with petrol. An alibi of sorts. Even though she's still got a good quarter of a tank left. The cop's stare remains stuck on her neck. It stings. Filling up with petrol is turning out to be an act of resistance. She calculates her gestures—insert card, key in password, unleaded fuel for the hybrid—then shakes the hose so as not to lose a drop, like her husband has taught her and like boys do with their dicks. She suddenly realises that she is the only woman here, apart from the cashier at La Croissanterie.

She gets back into the warmth of her car—warmth, everything is relative—but she's not about to start the motor, it's already easy enough to spot her. A golden light strikes the thoughtful brow of the cashier. Blond and Flemish in the shop window. Framed by the counter and the display stands, leaning over her cash register, she has the concentrated, almost solemn appearance of the milkmaid over her jug of milk, of the lace maker over her work, of the astronomer over his globe. Rose has the impression that the woman at the cash register of La Croissanterie is standing at the exact centre of the world. On the gap. Above the fault line. The crazy fault line. From where the prisoners are extradited. The inhabitants of the Earth are prevented at all costs from living there. She is at that precise spot where the planet forms a kink. It's not so much a matter of the sea or the cliffs, but a point where there's an obstruction in the terrestrial crust. Several spots like this can be found outside natural borders, but Calais has become a signifier. It's the very name of the obstacle.

The dinging of text messages. Younès! 'We are coming ☺' Rose smiled too. Then she frowned. 'We.' She was not about to pick up several people. Obviously. She was startled by a knock on the window. It wasn't Younès. A balaclava masking his face, a cop was gesturing for her to open the window. Fortunately she had all her registration and identity documents with her. Rose is always well prepared. The cop removed his balaclava to talk to her. He looked like Thomas Pesquet, the astronaut.

'What are you doing here?'

Admittedly, with a name like Goyenetche, she was a bit far from her habitat.

'I'm getting petrol.' She summoned up the exhilarating insolence of her teenage years. Rose Goyenetche has always had a problem with authority. While the cop studies her documents, she sees bits of her life flash before her, even though, come on, we're in a democracy here, she's not going to be shot or disappear, at worst she'd be held in custody, and on what pretext, hey? She's in a Total petrol station, in other words a public space, and also, along with cruise ships, one of the most consummate legal emblems of what capitalism represents.

Another guy arrived, greeted the cop—this petrol station was definitely the place to meet up. He said, 'Hello, Rose.' And then, turning to the cop, 'She's with us.'

'Ah, right,' said the cop.

The other guy was strikingly beautiful, long blond dreadlocks, the chiselled face of a rocker from the north of France. Rose felt her heart thumping, another life opening up, a glimpse of a future, however brief, in the arms of the rocker, that's all she needed right now. He was as commanding as the cop. He handed her a supermarket plastic bag through the window. 'Put that on.'

The two men leaned on the roof of her car. She heard 'We've got an injured guy', then 'hospital', and she had images of a truce during a war. She got out and pulled on the tunic from the Catholic Relief Services—way too big, the shoulders were enormous and there was almost a train at the back. So now she was endowed with a new gift. The cop gave her a mocking look.

'There's no fracture,' the dreadlocked guy said to her as if he was talking to a qualified nurse. 'We've got two third-degree sprains, one with torn ligaments, the other with a complete tear of the ligament and tibiotalar dislocation. I've got the X-rays. Let's go.'

'I'm not finished here,' said the cop.

In the bushes the border noises started up again, but he was only interested in her, or rather her car; he was walking around it, studying it carefully.

'Do you have the safety cap for the coupling device?'

The what?

'On the tow hook. The cap is mandatory. On the ball coupling.'

He was writing out a ticket. She was about to object—they'd been using the trailer for trips to Ikea—but the guy with dreadlocks pursed his lips.

'Driving offence, third class. On-the-spot fine, sixty-eight euros. The road-safety rules require that a vehicle must be of a high standard of roadworthiness, so as to reduce as much as possible, in the event of a collision, any risk of injury to human bodies. Turn on your headlights…You're missing at least five centimetres of the required ten metres vision in the front incline. Driving offence, third class. On-the-spot fine,

sixty-eight euros. Once you get a roadworthy certificate, report to the Calais police station, otherwise
your vehicle will be impounded. Article R313-3 of
the road-safety rules.'

'Can I report to another police station?' asked
Rose. 'Given that I have to attend to the wounded
person.'

'And where do you think you're going with your
pile of meat?' asked the cop.

She thought that was a funny way to describe her
perfectly decent car, her hybrid hire car. Then she
realised he was talking about the wounded person.
He was talking about the migrants.

Serge was the name of the guy with dreadlocks,
a name as old-fashioned as Rose. She followed him
without knowing where. He was walking fast, but
turned and smiled at her.

'He only wants you.' So Younès only wanted her.
It was some sort of consolation for two times sixty-
eight euros.

'He says you have something that heals.'

They came out of the circle of streetlights and
he switched on a torch. The wire fence had been cut
lengthwise. They were moving away from the border,
entering a nowhere zone of mud and gravel. Inside

the torch's yellow triangle, they moved towards the black background of the sky. She turned and stared at the Total petrol station as if it were a world unto itself, an aquarium of coloured lights. It was strange, that continuity: like rest areas on freeways, petrol stations are not isolated dots on vectors every few kilometres; they're part of the countryside.

Serge kept looking back at her, smiling exaggeratedly as if his hostage was going to escape. Fortunately she had seen enough news reports about the migrants to know that that wasn't what was going on at all. And, anyway, she'd follow this guy with the face of a broken angel to the ends of the Earth. Okay, that's enough.

At the end of the field they climbed a small embankment on the edge of the forest, this thing was turning into a proper hike, further along they came across slag heaps, no, they were huge piles of gravel or construction materials, and more and more stuff on the ground, plastic bags, lumps of cloth or whatever, cans, bits of packaging, and a trolley that must have been wheeled here in less muddy weather. Via a stretch of freeway, she had brought two climates into contact: she felt as if she still had one foot in the warmth, in Clèves' mild weather, but was also heading towards some indefinable state of mud and ice at Calais.

Now people were approaching. Behind the luminous beam of a phone, two men greeted them, good evening, good evening. Other figures hurtled down the hills, using phones to light their way. This was where they slept, on small shelves dug into the gravel, shipwrecked bodies in the walls of a north-facing hillside. And that gravel must be really hard to sleep on. An older man, with a red beanie, the spitting image of Captain Jacques Cousteau, came over to speak to them.

'She's the mother,' he said to other men behind him, hello, hello, she couldn't see their faces except in the flashes from the phones, just eyes and teeth. She had an easier time making out a young pink Englishwoman in a Care 4 Calais tunic, bonjour, hello.

There was a small fire crackling at the edge of the trees. A few people stood up, there were exclamations, more voices. Captain Cousteau, their guide, perhaps she should say their host, motioned for them to sit down on a pallet. They were all living in the woods. Like in the old days, she thought. Random reflections were passing through her mind. She was expecting to see camping tents or wooden huts and tarpaulins and lots of thick tape, like she had seen on photos of the notorious Calais Jungle. But there was nothing. Just two emergency blankets strung over the branches, scarcely even a gesture towards a tent.

A thermos arrived. Cousteau held out a beaker and poured her a steaming coffee. She wanted to see Younès but it seemed she had to drink coffee first. Serge took a beaker too. A set of hands passed her a plastic bag full of sugar. They were trying to make it easy by pouring the sugar for her; she was loath to say that she didn't take sugar. There were four or five people around her and she wanted to tell them not to worry about a spoon, but anyway a spoon appeared out of nowhere. She didn't understand what they were saying—in several languages, including French. She said thank you.

Where was Younès?

Others said to her, 'So it's good you came. May almighty God bestow peace, longevity and prosperity on you.'

'The rain really knocked us around,' explained Captain Cousteau. 'And we've been forced to pack up and leave so many times.'

A man showed her a sleeping bag stained with

something she couldn't identify, but which stung her nostrils horribly. Gas. They had been gassed. As soon as they set up a tent or the beginnings of a tent, they were made to clear out. They had been physically assaulted as well. The man pointed to his red eyes. She thought about the cop who had held the door open with that trusting, civilised, universal gesture: a man holds the door open for another man but then gasses him? Or else, are there two sorts of cops? Are there two sorts of men?

She realised that she had to finish her coffee and accept the Petit Lu biscuits from the Leader Price discount chain store before she could finally see Younès, before they would take her to him.

Next there was a lot of hustle and bustle; they were jostling, each one trying to show her the way. They had prepared everything: Younès was there beneath the improvised tent, those emergency blankets were definitely following him around—the blanket was his banner. He was lying on a sort of bed, buried in piles of blankets. He saw her and immediately looked away.

'Younès, say hello, it's Mum,' said Captain Cousteau.

'Hello,' mumbled Younès. He had grown

thinner, his skin stretched over his bones. He still had no front teeth. What was she expecting—kisses, emotional hugs, his teeth grown back? Couldn't he at least look her in the eye? There he was, wretched and broken. She was filled with a slightly inappropriate maternal rage: she had entrusted him to them and they were giving him back to her completely crippled. A survivor of a war she didn't want him to be part of, and from which no one had protected him. The other boys looked as if they were waiting for something. Well, she wasn't about to give a speech. She had to get him out of here.

There was a general move towards a trolley; they seemed to have got hold of one so they could push him back to the car park. In this mud? If that was the sort of thing they came up with to make it across to England, they wouldn't see the end of this any time soon. They were all talking now, nerves were fraying. But they must have discussed it all before, what to do, how to do it, all their differing opinions, her arrival must have been discussed, weighed up, rejected, desired, perhaps voted on, passed by a narrow margin.

Cousteau must have noticed her concern because he poured her another coffee and stood in front of her, screening her from the others. A woman appeared; it was the Nigerian woman. It suddenly struck her that they were all Nigerians. She asked Cousteau.

'No, I'm from Cameroon. The ones over there are Eritrean, that's why it's so hard to understand them.'

The Nigerian woman came over and held her hands. She was no longer wearing Gabriel's sweater, but she was thanking God for having brought Rose this far—yes, Rose, who understood only one in three words. She was thanking God and sobbing. Rose was so rattled that she wondered if young Younès might not have had some sort of liaison—on the cruise ship, or perhaps on the trawler and in the desert and before that—with this woman with the very large breasts, from whom he had not been apart until now. Rose was not about to take her as well. Another woman slipped into the light.

'She's Congolese,' announced Cousteau.

And she in turn was thanking the Virgin. 'May Mary be your guide and protect you against all evil, may she shelter you with her coat and may the warrior angels watch over you so that your car does not hit stones. The whole heavenly army is with you on this journey.'

Strange images were forming in Rose's tired brain: the Virgin Mary and a crowd of diaphanous angels sitting in the hybrid, fiddling with the GPS. She had to get going. Four strapping young men were milling around Younès, four for a coffin, she thought. She tried to brush off her anxiety as if it were a huge fly.

Outside—if you can say outside when it's just a sheet of plastic between you and out there—it started to rain. As if it wasn't already hard to hear, and now *rat-tat-tat*. Cousteau unfolded a brand-new rain poncho over Rose; he was adamant that it was a present. Meanwhile, the others were wrapping up Younès as well. They were both wearing bright red, no one would miss them.

'And where do you come from?' asked Cousteau, at once perfectly urbane.

'I'm from the Basque country.'

'That's right down south, isn't it?'

'Down the bottom to the west, before you get to Spain.'

Younès grimaced every time they touched his legs. Emerging from the hut, like a stretcher, was the entire bed—that method had won out—a bed that was a door, the lock still hanging off it. The four stretcher-bearers stepped gingerly out of the circle of light around the fire and moved under the blackness of the trees. As if by the magic of some state-of-the-art service, the white envelope of Younès's X-rays, stamped by the emergency department of the hospital in Calais, was placed on top of his legs. She followed the procession. She couldn't find Serge. Oh well.

Cousteau introduced himself. 'I answer to the name Mbiapep, Patience,' he said.

'I answer to the name Goyenetche, Rose.' She was adapting.

Part of the encampment was following; the no-man's land had become populated. A few of them had the same gloves attached to their belts that she had seen inside Younès's plastic bag at the Gare de Lyon. Whether it was fatigue or whatever, Rose had the feeling of already having witnessed this scene. The procession amid the torches, the bed being carried and the young man in pain, the cortege of dark figures. The picture remained in her mind. She stumbled. Patience held onto her.

'They're going to give it a try,' he said.

A try?

'Those guys have been trying to cross the border every night for days. Younès was following their example; that's how he fell off the truck. But thanks to your visit our spirits have been revived and you have motivated us to try again.'

The group broke into two, those who were going to try to cross, and those who, for now, were carrying. Those who were going to give it a try walked along by the wire fence towards the truck area; those carrying went out into the open with the bed, Younès on top. The cops looked on steadily. Patience explained that those trying to cross the border would try as many times as necessary until one of them snuck through. It was a numbers game, a single undetected person hidden in the back of a truck, getting through or dying, of asphyxia or of sorrow.

She opened the hybrid with her remote, *click*. She heard them commenting on the reliability, the fuel consumption and the design of cars like these. Then more discussions about whether they should get Younès to lie down on the back seat. That was the majority vote, but she wanted him in the front, seatbelt on, sitting next to her, and anyway it was her car, things were starting to get ridiculous. She tucked a rug around his legs. She remembered that she had brought along bags of clothes and blankets, on the off chance. She handed them out. She gave Patience a pair of shoes that were too small for her husband.

He thanked her for her contribution. 'For giving all of this to us, thanks to the love of God. This pair of shoes will remain of high significance in my journey. We live in a state of deprivation, once again thank you, we will always remain close to you.'

She shook his hand, unclear as to whether his bizarre way of expressing himself was simply his particular manner, or whether he was making fun of her, or if that was simply how things were done in his country. She was dumbfounded by the whole affair, right from the beginning.

The goodbyes took forever. Then she watched them calmly head towards the petrol station, perhaps to have a hot drink, or go to the toilet. They were neighbours, after all. Impassive on the passenger seat, Younès seemed to be gazing out at the road already. In the death seat, she thought. All they needed now was to have an accident. 'Not much sleep,' he said. They both took off their rain ponchos, a big mess of wet plastic. She started the engine, the doors locked automatically, and she finally felt herself again, in the family hybrid, with this boy she was carrying off. Goodbye, goodbye waves. Everyone in the small gathering responded, even the cop over there gave an ironic goodbye wave.

Younès had shut his eyes. She drove for a while. She stopped as soon as she felt she'd left the border area.

Her eyes shut.

When she woke up, it was daybreak. She felt weird. All tangled up. The tunic. From the Catholic Relief Services. She had forgotten to return it. It was very cold. Younès was still asleep. Her husband had left five messages. The car smelled of something odd. She smelled the tunic, discreetly sniffed Younès: a strong whiff of wood-fire smoke, of damp burnt wood. She had always associated the smell of wood fires with the comfort of home—in fact, it was the smell of anxiety and of being outdoors, the smell of the encampment. The same smell was on her.

Trucks came and went against a background of white frost. At the rest-area convenience store, she bought a bag of mass-produced croissants and a coffee for Younès with two sachets of sugar. He was awake. Inside the locked car, he looked worried and he groaned when he saw her. It was distressing. Then she realised that he needed to go to the toilet. It would be too hard for her to carry him by herself, into the men's area, and perhaps have to help him *inside* the toilets. Instead, she'd park over there, right at the end, by the interminable wire fences, over where the wild grasses were growing in the gap between the rest area and the farmland. He'd manage to piss out the door of the car. She walked away a short distance. The day had dawned properly now, it was freezing, she couldn't wait to get down south and away from all this.

Wedging himself back into a sitting position, the boy groans again. Rose hands him some wipes; they both clean their hands and face. There are still a few soot stains on his forehead, like a little chimneysweep. Inside his threadbare socks, his feet are swollen. Rose leans over, her long hair (because it's time to mention that Rose has long hair) falls over his face (like Mary Magdalene leaning over Christ, with or without the Catholic Relief Services tunic); she takes his ankles in her hands and Younès doesn't resist, the fluid—or whatever it is—is transmitted with unprecedented strength, Younès sighs, and when Rose sits up again everyone feels a lot better, and it's as if she's been fully recharged.

Younès was playing on the phone that used to belong to Gabriel. Not a huge fan of the passing landscape, even though he was being taken across the whole of France. She wanted to point out a few noteworthy things, if only the cows. Are there cows in Niger? She offered him chocolate, gave him some paracetamol, did nothing she would not have done with Gabriel. (Would she really have disturbed Gabriel for the cows? For the beauty of the Loire, yes, definitely.) He asked where they were going. They could have started with that. 'To Clèves,' she said.

They stopped at the rest area in Sainte-Maure-de-Touraine. They were a long way from any borders here; it was peaceful. She showed him the map of France on her phone, with Clèves down the bottom on the left. Younès zoomed in and out. She went into the Mie Câline bakery and bought a hamburger without bacon for him, a salad for herself and two Cokes, Light for her. Midday, nice weather. No one around. A Tuesday morning out of this world. The colourful playground in the rest area was sparkling after the recent rain. A light south wind blew. She needed a shower. He did too. She looked at him as he sat, dignified, in the reflection of the car windows. The shadows from the trees cast the outline of letters onto his forehead.

o

They are both eating in the car. He's being careful not to make a mess.

'It's not good,' he says.

The hamburger? No, where they were going. It was about time he started to worry about it.

'It's just until you get better,' says Rose. Saying it was a relief for her too.

A friend of his tried to cross the border at a Spanish port, he can't remember the name of it now. The friend had so many failed attempts at Calais that he'd gone that far south to try. Younès points to a spot on the map that could be Santander. 'We saw him when he came back to the encampment, exhausted, exhausted. You can't get through like that. No, you can't get through like that.' Younès clicks his fingers. There are star-shaped dots on them. 'It's the barbed wire,' he says. 'It shreds the gloves.'

He talks to her, but without looking at her. It's annoying. If Gabriel didn't look at her—but Gabriel is her son. If one of Gabriel's friends didn't look her in the eye, would she trust him?

'Look at me,' she says. She points to her eyes, her fingers in a V.

He looks at her. Then he lowers his eyes.

Does he have some kind of phobia?

He shrugs.

Is it something religious?

No.

But she is the Mum and you don't look older people in the eye.

She feels relieved. If that's all it is.

'Look at me when you speak to me. And don't call me Mum. My name is Rose Goyenetche. And yours?'

His name is Younès Aboussa. So.

IV

'You must change your life.'
Star Wars

Country people have no excuses whatsoever. Their houses are big. Younès is in the guest room. And, in any case, they would have rearranged the garage or the attic, a bed and extra heating, done. If necessary, they would have moved Emma into Gabriel's bedroom. Not Rose's consulting room, however—everything has just been set up, everything is ready.

Rose is bursting with energy. The guest room, with its own shower, is on the ground floor. Younès manages to get around on crutches. She bought him a stack of underwear, T-shirts, a pair of jeans, a new toothbrush, his own shampoo and soap, and a new case for his phone-that-used-to-be-Gabriel's, so that her son doesn't recognise the thing and call Younès a thief. The devil is in the detail. Rose is an organised woman. At the local practice the GP—who still has not referred a single patient to her, does he bear a grudge against shrinks?—examined Younès and studied the X-rays and was happy to work something out with the national health scheme; they're going to say that it was Gabriel with the busted ankles. Treatment: rest, compression, elevation with cryotherapy. Younès has to keep both feet elevated, his ankles wrapped in ice. The best thing, says the doctor, are packets of frozen peas. He'll be able to start physio as soon as the pain is more bearable. Lots of vitamins and calcium, fruit, fresh milk, pasta, rice, meat. We need to get this boy's strength up. Six weeks' treatment minimum, ideally three months'.

Come on, get a grip. She parks in front of the supermarket, leaves Younès in the car. They've run out of everything, no more milk, yoghurt, toilet paper, oranges, pasta, nothing. She's been gone for two days and it's as if a bomb has gone off in the house. Clothes everywhere, piles of dirty towels, the kitchen floor is sticky, the sink is blocked, all the lights have been left on. She buys two packets of frozen peas and an expensive air-freighted mango that will make the boy happy. She exchanges a few words with Delphine at the cash register. Delphine looks at Younès through the shop window.

'It's nice weather. I wonder if we'll have swallows this year,' says Delphine, as she scans the bag of oranges. 'Don't bother taking the milk out of the bag, it's okay, I've got it.'

'It's because of the pesticides. You're right, we never hear swallows anymore,' says Rose. 'But I saw three grey herons down near the banks of the Nive.'

'They're stuffing themselves with the last of the frogs,' says Delphine. 'All the frogs have got this horrible skin disease. So the herons get an end-of-days feast: frogs in their death throes. And the butterflies, remember the butterflies? They used to fly around those flowers we called windmills. When we walked home from school through the park'—Delphine turns towards the park, which is now a nursing home—'we heard the flowers whirring and the butterflies would land and leave powder on them, my mother said it was poison. That wasn't a hundred years ago, it was in the eighties.'

'You're right,' said Rose, 'I'd forgotten about all those butterflies.'

'They're not here and then we don't remember,' says Delphine. 'It's extinction.'

Delphine, who was once cute, has become enormous, probably from antidepressants. Rose holds out her credit card. Delphine looks at Younès, who is looking at his X-rays. He has even stuck them up on the windscreen so he can see them better, just like the doctor did on his lightbox.

Rose walks out, loaded up with the shopping, and stops dead in the supermarket car park. The opaque Younès is now transparent. Beneath his skin, deep down, are bones. Real bones. His skeleton and, inside it, death. That's what he's examining. Or he's examining life, the wonderful puzzle that is the human foot. The young Younès still has many steps ahead of him, on his soon-to-be-mended ankles.

Delphine is leaning against the window, leaving a halo of condensation, no doubt asking herself what on earth Rose is doing with the young black boy who is not getting out of the car. Delphine is married to the Kudeshayan son, whose father started the local grocery shop, and she has two mixed-race children, mixed-race Pakistani, as they say, in any case they're the only family like that around here. So if Delphine is asking herself questions, I don't know what they'd be, thinks Rose.

The whole family has started eating peas. Every day two packets of peas defrost around Younès's ankles, so they all adapt to it. By adding carrots, onions, lettuce, chicken. Younès has a healthy appetite, which is good to see. He's recuperating, he's on the mend. Rose is good at this: rehabilitating, reinforcing, tinkering so that things hold up. Christian points out that you could refreeze the same peas day after day, and not eat them. But even if they don't eat them, Rose is unnerved by the idea of breaking the cold chain.

Younès doesn't say anything at mealtimes. Perhaps where he comes from young people are not allowed to talk at the table. But he responds if he's spoken to. There's one thing that really annoys her: if he drops a bit of food on the ground, he apologises, picks it up, eats it, and apologises again. She tells him not to do that. The children will sweep up. The children are Gabriel and Emma, not him, if only because he can't walk at the moment.

Emma is always staring at him. Gabriel doesn't look at him. Emma asks him if you have to take a train to get to his country. Rose explains to Emma where Niger is and realises too late that she has not let Younès reply.

'Actually, Emma,' Rose adds, 'it's not on to ask where people come from.'

'I'm interested in where you're from,' says her husband, 'because I'd like to know who I've got living in my house, to get to know you and not "people".'

Younès seems a bit confused. Rose places her hand on her husband's hand. 'We're all from the same planet,' she says.

'Oh, for God's sake,' mutters Gabriel.

'Pardon?'

'Nothing,' says Gabriel.

Is Gabriel sulking? In any case, he's staying at the table, he's behaving properly, pouring water for everyone, and it's as if, thanks to the presence of a stranger, the whole family is behaving properly, no one looks scruffy, no one is swearing, and this magic seems set to last.

Younès eats everything but pork and especially likes rice lentils; he seems suspicious of certain vegetables (cauliflower, broccoli, fortunately not peas). As the first mango was a success, Rose buys more for him when she can find them at the supermarket (she hasn't gone back to the fruit-and-vegetable depot). One evening Younès cuts open the mango for the whole family and expertly removes the seed. She is about to show him how to cut it into cubes, like a hedgehog, but he already knows how.

'Where I come from, *kunu* is the word for hedgehog.'

Emma bursts out laughing. '*Cul nu*, naked bum, ha ha!' Gabriel snorts.

'What's the name of your language?' asks Rose, to change the subject.

'Zarma.'

'What?'

'It's one of the Songhay languages.'

'Ah.'

Younès smiles. 'I remember the mango rain. It arrives in the middle of the dry season, around March. Everything is covered in dust and a huge wind rises and a there's a massive downpour. It only lasts five minutes. But long enough to wash the mangoes, and afterwards they ripen. And everyone sleeps very well after this rain.'

Rose likes the sound of the mango rain. It's the first mention he's made of his country, or should she say his past. She pictures an uncertain landscape, half-wet, half-desert, a shower of rain curtaining the mangoes. But what does a mango tree look like? She can see two oak trees through the bay window of her new consulting room. And she pictures the Niger

River, which she has traced via satellite image and which spreads out like a boa constrictor, its rounded back beneath the Sahara.

She and Younès are drinking coffee in her consulting room, on the ground floor of the house, with its own separate entrance and certificate from the social-security collection agency. The poster of the Mondrian exhibition at the Pompidou Centre needs to be hung, but Rose is not sure now—is it too Parisian? For the sake of convenience, she has set Younès up on the couch, both feet elevated on a cushion. But it's not at all like being with a patient. And anyway, Emma is here, curled up at the bottom of the couch. It's more like the beginning of a story.

'Can you swim in the Niger?' Rose asks.

'Yes,' he says, 'It's nothing like training in a swimming pool, but it's good enough for learning to swim.'

'Are there crocodiles?' asks Emma.

'I've never seen any in Niamey, but I've often seen hippopotamuses—they're very dangerous.'

'Hippopotamuses!' screams Emma.

'You have to swim near the rocks because the hippos don't like them. They cut their skin. Hippos once tipped over a school transport vehicle, a canoe full of children, who all drowned, twenty of them.'

'A canoe!' shouts Emma.

'Occasionally there are very big sea cows, which are completely harmless, we eat them. Every Friday, I used to swim in the pool of the Terminus Hotel with my uncle. It's the best pool in Niamey. Adults go there to drink Conditions.'

'What's that?'

'Beer—the price fluctuates depending on the economic…conditions.'

Rose laughs with Younès. Emma remains solemn. Rose looks out her bay window and tries to visualise those Muslim people drinking beers by the hotel pool.

Younès is losing his accent. He's trying hard to swallow his *r*s in the back of his throat. He's copying Gabriel's intonation. Rose takes him in the car when she goes shopping or when she picks up Emma—it gets him out of the house. It gets him used to Europe, even; it gets him in training for later, she tells herself. She is continually showing him things, explaining things. It worries her husband, but there are never any police checks on these roads, not since the days when there were still Basque terrorists. And he talks in the car. It has become their favourite activity: the two of them in the long lines of traffic jams, each looking ahead at the road; it's easier for talking. She tells him bits and pieces about her childhood; they pass her old school, which is now the town hall, and the court where they still play pelota. In Niamey he went to a private school run by an Iranian. His uncle paid the fees. But at university not a single computer worked. And after university there were no jobs. There was no electricity at home unless the generator was working.

'There is no running water like here. You have no idea,' says Younès, matter-of-fact. He adjusts the air conditioning so it blows on his face. His uncle has a beautiful house. He was famous, a singer, a well-known Nigerien musician.

'And then he died, and it was not good.'

'So that's why you left?'

'My aunt paid for the trip. She made me promise not to go by boat. But Libya was not good.'

It's clear that he does not want to talk about Libya. He looks out at the landscape here, the reassuring landscape, thinks Rose, with its roads that lead from the supermarket to the post office, its sculptured verges, its roundabouts, where there is no chance of Libyans suddenly leaping out. Rose tries to imagine a jumble of cowboys and Indians on the wonderfully peaceful rolling green landscape of her childhood, with its deep layers of soil, full of her roots.

'How are you?' asks her mother. 'And how is our Younès?'

'Younès is resting in his room, he's fine, fine.'

For the first time, Rose has some young patients coming this Wednesday afternoon when there is no school, so her mother is taking Emma to the beach. Rose wraps up Emma's snack, gluten-free soybean biscuits.

'From time immemorial,' says her mother, 'man has thrived on wheat and milk.'

It's an hour's drive to the sea, which worries Rose. And they'll eat defrosted quiches, the bacon bits exuded from under the skin of who knows what poor pigs. And the sweets! Rose visualises these products of a cynical economy breaking through the immune defences of her daughter like invisible aliens.

'The terrorists attacks and all that are terrible, aren't they?' says her mother.

'Terrible,' agrees Rose.

'And you're putting up a Muslim.'

'What's does that have to do with anything?' asks Rose, motioning to her mother to lower her voice.

'So he's not Muslim?'

'If only we didn't despise Arabs so much,' whispers Rose. 'And anyway he isn't Arab. You're making me talk rubbish.'

'So we're the ones with the Kalashnikovs now?'

Her mother says Kalashnikovs as if the object had become an everyday thing, as if she had gone off and fought in the secret service as soon as she'd been able to get Rose into kindergarten. Here we go again, they're arguing.

'Your generation had everything: retirement, a national health scheme, contraception without AIDS, a long enough time between wars to play around in, only small terrorist attacks, plenty of leisure, and now the planet is in a filthy state because you spent your life living it up.'

'All the same, I paid for your cruise!'

Rose refrains from holding forth on that vessel of floating capitalism, those tonnes of shit motoring around at full speed. She makes them both a coffee, using fair trade beans, and changes the conversation to the weather, but the weather is also a hot topic, because Rose's mother remains a climate-change sceptic.

○

It's raining, so tourists attend the open-for-inspections. Her husband is tired. All day long, young couples turn up at the real-estate agency, along with retired couples, families, single people. Their umbrellas and dogs drip everywhere and they ask to see the two-bedroom apartment, the studio with the view, or the villa worth three million. House inspections are a hobby, an entertainment for the locals. In Paris only nutcases go in for that and you can pick them easily.

The other illness endemic to this place is crazy overvaluation. Thirty years in the same home, children gone, they decide to sell, they think people will pay dearly for this house that is so close to their hearts. Or they inherit from grandma and believe that places in the countryside are worth an arm and a leg because prices on the coast have skyrocketed, and they persist in overvaluing their hovels that have been languishing on the market for an eternity. And who do they blame? The real-estate agent.

Her husband pours himself another drink. And yet he still believes in the ideal agency, like a dating service between places and lives. He dreams of starting his own; the logo would be a hermit crab, which changes its shell as it grows…But here they insist he works around the clock to make sales.

His boss is worse than his boss in Paris. Today they did an exercise in order to ramp up their performance. They ranked the clients: Don Quixote or Sancho Panza, risk or security. You have to sell the purchase to the purchaser the way you sell the sale to the seller. The way you sell the therapy to the patient! Her husband drains his glass and hiccups, laughter or tears, she can't tell.

And that's not the end of the NLP, the neuro-linguistic programming, either. There's mirroring. Your client crosses his legs, you cross your legs. Your client turns to face you, you lean towards him. He looks out the window, you sell him the dream! The aim is for him to recognise you. It's you. He's found you. He is going to *prefer* you, because you're his exclusive agent. Rose visualises her husband's windowless office—oh, no, that was in Paris. Here at least he has a window, a proper office near the station. Admittedly they're still a long way from a view of the sea.

They're drinking whisky on the terrace. It's already hot and humid. Younès is upstairs, asleep perhaps, while Gabriel is writing (he actually seems to have started a novel), while Emma is no doubt scratching herself; her eczema is not getting better, there's nothing to be done with this child, with or without the magic of the countryside it's getting worse, it's as if a swap took place on the Acropolis and they got an inferior version of her.

'Perhaps it's because we moved,' says her husband.

'Ah, no,' says Rose. 'If you don't take a risk, you'll never do anything.'

Her old friend Nathalie has a nice physiotherapy practice in a small building near the pelota court, but the fountain in the shape of a gurgling Buddha is a bit unexpected. Same for the framed posters of polished stones and orchids. Rose definitely prefers her Mondrian. Nathalie holds out her hand to shake Younès's, but he doesn't reciprocate. What's he up to? He looks at Rose, pleading.

What brought that on? After the moment of embarrassment in the delicately perfumed atmosphere and the zen music, after the moment of general awkwardness, what made Younès not want Nathalie to touch him? Hey?

He says he doesn't need it. And anyway he doesn't know her.

How come? What, with a double sprain, he doesn't need it and doesn't know her?

'You,' says Younès, suddenly using the familiar form of address, and speaking only to her, 'you are the Mum who heals.'

Rose shakes her head, upset. 'It's all a bit complicated to explain.'

'There's nothing to explain,' says Nathalie. 'Is it because I'm a woman?'

'That's not at all what he said,' says Rose. 'I should have spoken to him about it earlier. We can still talk about it.'

Younès waits, silent, while the two women have their heated exchange. They go out on the balcony of the consulting room. Nathalie lights a cigarette.

'I don't know how you can accept that,' says Nathalie. 'You're the feminist in the village, you and your mother.'

'Don't confuse things,' says Rose.

'*Actually*, I am not confusing things,' says Nathalie. 'He didn't even look at me.'

'It's a misunderstanding,' says Rose.

'All the same, there are things we care about in this country,' says Nathalie. 'As for the idea that *everything is equally valid*. I'm not a psychologist…'

'What do you mean, everything is equally valid and you're not a psychologist?' says Rose. 'And where did you get the idea that everything is equally valid for psychologists?'

'Well, anyway,' spits Nathalie, 'let me tell you, there's no way you'll get any clients if that's how you treat them.'

(A typical act of projection: Rose had gathered that Nathalie didn't have many clients.)

Okay, let's go. Rose had never really liked Nathalie anyway. She gets annoyed as she helps Younès into the car: the seatbelt jams and her phone rings. It's Nathalie. Speak of the devil.

'You forgot his X-rays. You need to know, Rose: this guy is at least twenty or twenty-five years old. It's been a long time since he's had a growth plate in his bones.'

Rose rings off. She tries to think if there's another physio nearby, a man perhaps? She looks at Younès, this young adult, this stranger, who in turn is looking her straight in the eye.

The good thing is that they can wear shorts almost the whole year round, a pelota bat slipped into their wicker basket, just in case. And the local macho guys don't mind wearing pink or baby blue, with a little cashmere sweater knotted over the Lacoste polo shirt. It's nice. You can breathe in this place. The Goyenetche family have modified their wardrobe. Occasionally a raincoat, but never a parka, except when the foot of the Pyrenees turns white, one or two days a year, and except for Younès, who is always bundled up in his woollen layers like an old woman.

At least two months, says the new physio, in a pink polo shirt, one of the Villebaroin cousins in South B, who is also happy to work out something with Gabriel's national health registration because it's the first time he's been able to help a migrant, we don't have many of them here, we don't think of the Spanish and Portuguese like that anymore, and even we Basque people have migrated a lot, haven't we?

Good man. They have to drive there and back three times a week for rehab.

'That's a long way, isn't it, from Clèves?' he says.

'Oh no, not at all, I don't mind.'

It's Younès who needs persuading: 'Younès, I'm treating you, okay,' she says, 'but you *also* need physiotherapy.'

At least two months before they know if he's better, by which time it will almost be summer.

o

So she places her hands on his ankles. They are sitting calmly in her consulting room and she can feel the swelling and the heat under her palms. The swelling is going down quickly, day by day. That's normal, right, with the physio and the frozen peas? Younès wiggles his toes with pleasure.

Leaning on her arm, he tries out a few steps on the terrace. They've installed a perfectly decent DIY swimming pool in the garden, where you can do three breaststrokes lengthwise and two across. Younès trusts her to set him up on the edge of the pool so he can wiggle his feet in the water. It's good for him, but he shivers, Clevès' southern sun is not enough for him. We are always north of where someone else comes from.

She is starting to see a few patients, mostly referred by her Parisian colleagues. Here she only knows people from her childhood, and clearly that's not the best recommendation. And she knows there's gossip about her and her migrant. Once the patients leave, she hears the tapping of crutches on the terrace and he goes and sits in his favourite spot, in front of the pool, looking out at the Pyrenees. Headphones on, he moves his head, even his feet, to the rhythm. He's like a passenger on a stopover.

She would have liked to take charge of his life, fill out his application for asylum, write his story and send it to the French Office for the Protection of Refugees and Stateless Persons. She got all the information, she contacted the local branch of the Catholic Relief Services, and France Land of Asylum, she is the full bottle on the rights of unaccompanied minors, she is super up-to-date about it all, the bone measurements thing is meaningless, it dates back to the bad old days in the thirties. So she would have liked to organise his future in a better way than through his ankles, help him to get across borders in another way.

'But you're helping me,' he insists.

His young hand is resting on her shoulder like a bird. He takes one step, two steps, three steps, he lets go, he walks forward like a tightrope walker, he is standing up on the Earth. She would like to infuse him with more than his newfound walking ability. She would like to transmit to him the power to follow whichever meridians he chooses.

They no longer refer to it as the guest room but as Younès's room. You have to knock first. It's all very well for her to admit that he needs his privacy and that it's his own space, but when he calls out 'Come in', like some nabob, she gets annoyed. There are no nabobs in Niger, so a sultan or a Fulani prince or however she imagines them. She picks up a towel off the floor, she gives him his clean bed linen, she tells him to sort out his own dirty clothes and to put them in the washing machine himself. Honestly! He's in the shower for hours and it's like a lake in there when he leaves the bathroom. After all, he could just use the mop, couldn't he? Despite his ankles, it's surely not beneath his dignity. So, just like Gabriel.

Sometimes she finds him in the laundry looking at the clothes tumbling in the washing machine. It's touching. And he loves heating milk for himself in the microwave. He watches the bubbles forming and then *ding*, he presses on the stop button just before the milk overflows. His room is filled with Gabriel's things, and Christian's, he has almost nothing that belongs to him but she can already see the void he will leave, it will be hard to believe when he's gone. It will always be Younès's room.

On the internet, he shows her videos of his uncle Sani. There are only two of them. Joyful music but serious singers, a solemn drummer, long point collars and a grainy image, Africa of the independence movement, Africa of the future back then. The young uncle looks like Younès, a good-looking kid, wearing an embroidered cap, performing a melancholy dance, stylish, a cross between Fela Kuti and Ali Farka Touré, with a nod to Bob Marley. She sways as she listens. Who would have thought Niger could be so festive. Well, it was a long time ago, back when she was listening to Supertramp in Clèves.

After the physio sessions at South B, she invariably takes him to look at the sea. Often after the sessions he sulks, complaining that they do him more harm than good. She parks at the casino and, prudently, he walks the fifty metres to Glaces Lopez with her. He always has vanilla-chocolate and refuses to taste the other 'preposterous' flavours. Lopez likes the word, so always gives him an extra scoop or a cigarette wafer, a novelty for Younès—he has fun pretending to smoke it, joking around, like Emma used to do with the same biscuits on the cruise. With his missing teeth he looks like a child. He is in awe of the alarming strength of the waves. 'I will never swim here!' Rose feels a pang of emotion: one day she would like to welcome him here as a legal, relaxed tourist. The first time he saw the sea was in Libya. He was shocked by the taste of it, *ache dey*! 'It's not salty like the water in a cooking pot, it's a huge gathering of fish.' He squints as he eats his ice-cream. He says he had to force himself to *leave his feet*, but he was frightened. So he had to start swimming training. He shakes his head. She thinks back to the horribly black sea at night during the cruise. She would like to cure him of those memories.

'Niger is a magnificent country,' he says. 'The most beautiful country in Africa. You should go there one day. When you're in Niger, that's when you see the Sahara properly. But the heat makes you sick. It's often forty-five degrees. A child leaves its mother's womb with a temperature of thirty-seven degrees, so it's much higher. Here it's cold, but you can breathe.' Gracefully, with both hands, he waves the sea air onto his face. 'And also, in Niger,' Younès adds wearily— as if he really had to explain the reasoning behind his situation?—'in Niger there is *nothing*.'

His phone beeps. *Tssiii tssii tssii*. She's come to hate that insect noise. That's the end of their moment of grace. The story is interrupted. The young man is preoccupied, swallowed up by another space. He answers the phone. Someone replies. *Tssiii tssii tssii*. Often, when he's alone, she can hear him on the phone. Is he calling the Nigerian woman?

o

Wild geese have been flying over the village since this morning. They're coming back from Morocco. Their cry is very recognisable, a sort of hoarse trumpeting that gets Rose out of bed. She is in her childhood garden, madcap, flying around with the geese. Then, just like in her childhood, gunshots destroy the peace. The triangular formations disband, the panic-stricken geese search for each another, there's one, then two, then three, reconstituting one point and the triangle spreads out like a vapour trail, then hits a wall of gunshots, and off it goes again, the hunters versus the birds. And all day long the geese will struggle, circling the village, which has become impassable. She should call the cops, but the cops around here are also hunters. She could just imagine the chaos, Rose and her migrant, the hunters and their guns.

Emma is singing:

> *Deer, deer, open up!*
> *Or the hunter will kill me.*
> *Rabbit, rabbit, enter, come in,*
> *And shake my hand.*

Arnaud has come over for a drink. He comes over a lot, too much perhaps. He's still got his idea of going into partnership with her. He claims that, in the past, the simple touch of her hands used to make him less stupid. She gives him a stern look: stop it! According to Arnaud, time does not exist in the astral world. Apparently, he explains, the people around here have a particular disposition towards *pareidolia*, seeing faces in random shapes. The area is humid and conducive to the formation of moulds and dark stains: the dead return through walls, people see the faces of those who are missing.

'In other words,' says Rose, 'families who refuse the benefits of psychology are more inclined to produce individuals who are open to witnessing supernatural phenomena?'

'That's it,' says Arnaud. 'Sometimes, in order to speak of the dead, the only solution is to see them.'

Younès, sitting further along on the terrace, looks up from his phone. He must think they're quite eccentric. Arnaud and he look at each other across the gulf of their differences.

'In the future,' Arnaud calls out, 'Rose will perform miracles.'

Younès smiles amiably.

In the meantime, Arnaud tells them, he is looking after a neighbouring family who are besieged by a ghost. See, the people who put their trust in healers, clairvoyants, medicine men, magicians, witches are more numerous than whatever Rose was told at school, at hospital, at work, in all those places where you have to toe the line.

The gunshots start up again around the house, it's the war against animals. The three of them lower their heads when a hail of lead shot strikes the albizia tree. 'Assassins!' yells Arnaud. He raises his fist against the invisible attackers. As an adolescent Arnaud behaved like a shit, especially with Solange. But perhaps the only true division in the world is between those who are willing to kill and the others. And anyway, he behaves well with Younès. Neither condescending nor indiscreet, he's attentive, taking an interest in how his ankles would have been cared for back home ('Only if you've got the money—same as here!' laughs Younès), curious about Rose's technique, the way she moves her hands around the damaged area. 'Essentially, Younès is your guinea pig.' It's her turn to laugh; she's embarrassed.

Younès moves his chair into the light. It's that time of day when the sun is about to disappear behind the mountains, when they'll shut the patio doors, perhaps even light a fire. They are all alive, here in this comfortable part of the world, in houses that are well ventilated in summer and well heated in winter.

Today it rained on the mangoes in Niamey; his mother sent him a video. Huge green leaves are thrashing around frenetically, the beaten red earth seems to be thumping, and there's the hut where the caretaker has taken shelter. So they have a caretaker. And his mother knows how to send videos.

'The chickens have also taken shelter,' Younès points out. 'My mother keeps lots of chickens and we also keep goats. The neighbours find it a lot fascinating, as they don't have any, or maybe only a few.'

Rose laughs. 'You don't say *a lot fascinating*; you say *very fascinating*.'

Younès disputes that you say *very fascinating*. Perhaps he's right.

'Do you miss your mother?' Rose asks.

Younès sighs. 'Yes, her I miss a lot.'

I'll set his French right another time, thinks Rose.

When she massages his ankles—yes, let's call it a massage—it's more like what you'd traditionally call the laying on of hands, like Saint Louis beneath his oak tree in Vincennes (unless she's confusing it with his work as a judge). Whatever, it's a matter of allowing her hand to act, hot, supple, suffused with power. Sometimes Younès falls asleep. Sometimes she encourages him to talk about his mother; a little bit of healing happens that way. His mother had never countenanced him going away—'Why are you always dreaming of leaving?'—and had tried to stop him by barring the door, but he got past anyway. He never speaks about his father. He talks about the garri flour grains his mother gave him for the trip, more garri than an elephant could eat.

'I took the bus from Niamey to Agadez, twenty-two thousand francs for a ticket, we left at eight in the morning, but we didn't arrive until nine at night because after Abalak the bitumen has disintegrated: they call the road "Choose your hole". After Agadez, I was in a ten-wheeled Mercedes Thirty-Two. It only went on sand. I had a spot in the driver's cabin; it was very expensive, paid for by my aunt. The others paid eighty-five francs and were lashed onto a load of cigarettes and cola nuts. The sea is terrifying, but the desert is *riskful* too, especially if the driver is one of those amateurs who loses his passengers. But a professional people-smuggler does a good business per head.'

Rose's whole being is in her hands. Her breath,

her energy, her silence have focused themselves there. She has discovered that she listens better that way, her hand connected not to her head but in a way to Younès's, the ankle nothing more than a contact point.

'At Agadez the driver was from Toubou, then it changed to another one at the Ténére Tree, then again at Dirkou, then again at Madama. We unloaded the cola nuts, those nuts that taste so bitter at first, then deliciously sweet, and keep you awake. Every change of driver took a long time. We stopped in Tourayet for two days, waiting for cigarettes. The water supply diminished: I had a two-litre container and a smaller one. Water is something you don't give away; you give it to your brother, except if you have hardly any left, and you don't sleep, otherwise someone might steal it from you. At Toumo, just past the border with Libya, we were in a Land Cruiser ute and we hadn't slept because we were frightened of falling out of the ute. We were held in a military camp for a long time. They hit me, they tore up the photo of my girlfriend, and they took the good-luck charm my mother had sewn for me, they considered it haram, forbidden by Islamic law, even though they let the Nigerian prostitutes through.'

So he had a girlfriend? And what about the Nigerian woman, then? Did he meet her back there? She tries to remember everything he's telling her: if he tells it all to the authorities, he's sure to get asylum, isn't he?

'The Ténére Tree is frightening from a distance; it looks like a jinn. It was an acacia, the most isolated tree on Earth. A drunk Libyan driver knocked it down. Now there's just a metal antenna with a kind of head, standing in the middle of the desert, a memory of a tree where there is no longer a tree at all.'

Emma's eczema has become like a part of her, and despite the good air she constantly has a blocked nose. The paediatrician (they have to go to South B and it's almost impossible to find a park) prescribed a battery of tests. When she opens the mail, Rose learns that her daughter is allergic to albizia, wormwood, birch, chestnut, oak, oleander, lily, hazel tree, dwarf palm, bluegrass and willow. They have to demolish the whole garden. She had a vision of the famous little Vietnamese girl running naked through a landscape of burning napalm.

Younès has offered to babysit Emma after school. Which means Rose can take on more patients. He gets her to do her homework and teaches her words from his language: *ni kani baani*, how are you; *ay gono*, I am here; *fofo*, hi. *Fofo, fofo!* The little girl repeats it endlessly.

One evening after working late, she finds them watching *E.T.*, sharing a packet of Prince chocolate biscuits on the couch.

'I am zypnotising you,' says Emma, and Younès drops down dead.

Emma jumps for joy. 'You have to shake him to wake him up!'

Gabriel stays locked in his room. They call him at meal times, *dinner's ready!*

They encourage Younès to join in the family conversation, and Younès, like E.T., talks only of leaving. It's frustrating. London this, London that. So many promises. God save the Queen. Apparently there are no police checks of identity documents anywhere in England, and finding a job is a piece of cake. He watches *E.T.* in the original, so he can improve his English.

All Gabriel thinks about is Paris. Rose feels surrounded by extraterrestrials. Next year Gabriel will sit his baccalaureate and then we'll see...we'll see what? She stops herself from comparing Gabriel and

Younès, but everyone knows what she's thinking. The party boy and the adventurer. The Prince and the Pauper. Even if she'd never wish Younès's fate on her son in a million years.

Gabriel objects once too often that his jeans are being pinched, so on a Saturday morning she cancels her consultations in order to take Younès to the H&M in North B. She has to drag him out of bed like the adolescent he still is, routinely missing his morning prayer, not that it seems to bother him; he'd like to do his midday prayer, but hang on, no, stop, we're leaving, off to H&M right now, otherwise we'll hit the traffic. The main road is already packed.

At Decathlon he chooses boots that provide good support for his ankles, good footwear for *giving it a try*. Rose doesn't need him to spell it out. He tells her that a guaranteed border-crossing place is ten thousand euros, the 'embassy' rate where you leave from Paris by car. For eight thousand euros you leave from Calais; it's riskier, but if that doesn't work out you can try again as many times as you need. For three thousand euros you get three attempts in a truck. The lowest rate is five hundred euros: the people-smuggler guarantees only that the truck is opened and then locked with the correct seal. It's like a Starbucks menu, there are so many options: she can't get over the multiple-choice aspect of the border-crossing business. Crossing by yourself takes time, at least six months in Calais, and if you're given the once-over by the cops or the people-smugglers, you have to head to Dunkirk or Belgium or even the Netherlands. But from Calais *you can see England*.

They get back on the main road. There you go, the traffic is coming to a standstill.

His grandmother lives in Arlit. 'You should come,' says Younès. 'They say Arlit is the second Paris.'

A truck cuts across in front of Rose, she brakes and has the same reflex she has with her children: she reaches her hand out as if she was stronger than a safety belt, stronger than death.

'Bring the whole family,' says Younès. 'There's a direct flight to Niamey. The most beautiful dunes in the Sahara are in Arlit. You can stay as long as you like at my grandmother's.'

'The French hostages stayed three years,' says Rose.

'There is no danger at all with my grandmother offering you hospitality.'

Rose imagines a Nigerien grandmother; she does her best to imagine one, half-Tuareg, half-Marguerite

Duras, tattooed all over and gifted with superpowers, standing up, all by herself, to the jihadists of al-Qaeda in the Islamic Maghreb. And she thinks about the superpower contained in her passport, and about this kid inviting her, and she shakes her head. Even though, off we go, in one flight, one visa stamp, she could be there after a few hours above the clouds, sea and desert, and it would make Younès so happy, and she could go and visit his mother, his aunt and his grandmother and, he urges, she would be received like a queen.

'Let's not get too carried away,' says Rose.

In the end it's just a dream made of sand and dunes, a mirage to be precise. She recalls their one and only plane trip—Christian, Gabriel, Emma and her—to Los Angeles. Solange had sent her four Air France tickets for a film premiere, of which Rose has absolutely no memory. Rose in the plane, stuffed with tranquillisers and squeezing her husband's hand for twelve hours. The whole trip was ruined by the vision of the mangled bodies of her children in the debris of the cabin, her whole Californian holiday overshadowed by the terror of having to get back on the plane. The five-hour train trip from Clèves to Paris is just fine.

○

The seven-year-old boy is suffering from a shocking case of shingles. The parents have tried everything; they are even ready to accept a psychological hypothesis, so they have come to see her, Madame Rose Goyenetche. They don't like shrinks, but apparently she is special and her name is from around here and that's reassuring. An intense pain has lodged itself in the child, in the area of his shingles band. The blisters have left a red rash all along his diaphragm, right around his body, and that's not good at all, thinks Rose. It's the sort of pain that leaves no room for life, an incomprehensible, arbitrary, meaningless pain that drives you crazy. The mother is pale and thin, the father looks away, the family is only connected by the thread of an unbearable here and now. No question of the little boy drawing, and don't even think about him kneading a bit of playdough. Even sitting on a chair is unbearable. What she can deduce from his groaning is that the pain manifests itself as frequently repeated sets of electric shocks; even the slightest movement means he is in its grip. At best his future is catatonia. All the GP does is prescribe him paracetamol—unbelievable. The closest neurologist is in Bordeaux, the next available appointment in six months' time.

She lies him gently on the couch. She asks the parents to leave the room. She hums a nursery rhyme to him in Basque, the one about loving a bird, the bird flying away. She makes up the words she can't remember; she gives free rein to her intuition like she used to in the good old days with Bilal and Grichka.

'Your head is heavy,' she murmurs, to reassure herself as well, 'your shoulders are heavy, your arms are heavy, your elbows, your wrists, your chest and your whole tummy.'

The child's body resists, his face is going to contort, and Rose feels the pain like a crouching beast, right there, between her and the child, ready to leap up and bite, but she intervenes. She draws herself up into the pose of a horse Jedi; fortunately no one is watching, except the boy. The beast retreats. She takes on another pose. She carries out the final expression of the movement, and the little boy's gaze gives her strength. She dances. A smile hovers around the boy's lips. She takes him in her arms. He doesn't groan. He clings on to her, and she performs that ancient gesture: she carries him. She lifts him off the ground. The boy slumps, and his clenched muscles go slack. She takes nine steps across the room, over to the wall, she turns around, this room drawn up by instinct on the plan turns out to be exactly the right size, she takes nine steps in the other direction. The vibrating thread that held him to the ground gives way with a snap that courses through her body as if she's been whipped. She is stunned. Everything unwinds. She puts him on the ground, on his feet. He raises his head. The pain has left him. The pain has gone back to crouch among the shadows, over where the night resides.

'The question,' says her husband, 'is not how long he stays, but how long can we accommodate him properly?'

'The question,' she corrects him, 'is how long he will agree to stay.'

The more damaged ankle has still not regained its flexibility, but he's now walking without crutches. He spends hours playing games on the Wii; it's excellent for balance and for all the little muscles and tendons, the sural nerve in the calf, the posterior hamstring, the tibiotalar joint, and the anterior sheath that attaches in front of the talus. Don't think for a moment that Rose isn't the full bottle on anatomy.

What's more, she's going to get his teeth fixed. There is no dentist in Clèves, but the physio in South B, the one always in the pink polo shirt, has recommended a mate whose clinic is near the station. Her husband will take him, as it's right near his office. Younès is going to need several appointments, two incisors and a canine tooth, if you can believe it, two casts for pivot crowns, fairly major reconstruction work. Younès is fine about it. It's booked in for next month, and it'll cost an arm and a leg, but Rose has taken on more and more patients.

She uses her hands as much as her words now, and the patients are fine without words. With her husband encouraging her and Arnaud still keen to join forces, it's starting to go to her head. Now she greets the GP with a degree of arrogance: she does things that he doesn't know how to do with his pen and his prescriptions. Okay, she shouldn't get ahead of herself.

Younès is learning to ride a bike. The physio said there was nothing better for ankles than bike riding. Younès refuses to give any credit to the physio but is happy to try the bike, in order to keep building up his strength, as he says. Rose sighs as she contends with this would-be He-Man who wants to *try* again. The bike would allow him, heaven knows, to do all sorts of other things, be independent, get to the drop-in legal-aid centre at the Catholic Relief Services, begin procedures with the local administrative centre, and hand in his case history to the refugee-protection office. Right?

At first Younès treats the bike like an enemy creature. When he tries to climb on top of it in an uncharacteristically clumsy way, Emma bursts into laughter. Rose wonders whether the boy is perhaps uncoordinated after all, not at all suited for crossing the border to England. Do they know exactly how he fell off that truck? She has visions of him hidden in the boot of the hybrid, packed under umpteen blankets, no, no, no, that would be too dangerous, there are too many stories on the internet, too many good souls—and she means that without a hint of irony—worthy citizens who end up in prison trying to reunite families via the Channel, that stretch of water that has for so many become like the DMZ between the two Koreas.

'It's normal to defend your border,' says Younès, whose opinion she hadn't sought. 'It's for your own security. I've been there: no security is no good.'

More and more now, he talks to her as if she was

a clueless woman. She's going to put him in his place.

'The world is ruled by irrationality. So much poverty in the south; only the rich have identity papers; the bottleneck at Calais and the nightmare of those metal gates; the planet is being destroyed; fascism is on the rise, and you want cops so this system stays in place?'

'I want the same security you have.'

'But do you have family in London?' She's starting to think that perhaps the Nigerian woman got through, and he wants to meet up with her. She's annoyed by the thought, and annoyed that she's annoyed.

He makes no answer.

'Don't you think your British magic kingdom is a bit overrated?'

'Nigeriens hardly ever migrate,' Younès concedes in a thoughtful tone, as if it was some sort of explanation.

'We unloaded the cola in Qatrun, an oasis held by the Toubou people. Further north, in Sabha, there was an airport. I wanted to go to Tripoli, nine hundred kilometres away, the same distance as from Niamey to Agadez. But I'd run out of money. In Sabha I spent days watching planes take off.'

Rose checks that her phone is recording properly. She hasn't given up on the idea of writing down his life story, for his asylum case.

'I stayed in a house rented by some Zarma people and some Hausa people. Only men. They traded in food and cigarettes. Two Chadian guys helped me; they gave me beans for breakfast. I can speak a bit of Hausa, so the Hausa guys translated into Zaghawa for the guys from Chad, who replied in English and then we went back into Hausa.

'I decided to head for Tripoli, whatever it cost. I was the only one to have left with suitcases, which had already got a laugh from everyone on the truck. I sold my clothes. That got a laugh from the guys from Chad too. But I still didn't have enough for a plane ticket. That cost my aunt another hundred thousand francs for me to travel illegally to Tripoli. In a Daewoo four-wheel drive. They put me up front, completely veiled except for one eye. One of Gaddafi's ex-bodyguards was the people-smuggler who organised the deal. Arab people are *habituated* to spend the weekend with their families, like white people do, so they put printed clothing fabric over the windows to give the impression there were other women behind. I crouched down as much as I could in the front. I was already tall. There were three militia checkpoints on the way to Tripoli. I prayed. I was frightened. One checkpoint. Two checkpoints. As soon as the guards saw women, we got through. I pretended I was old, I trembled, I shook my head. The four guys on the back seat were shoving each other because there was no room. At the third border checkpoint, there was banging on the boot. "Open up! Open up!" I thought there were six of us, but we were nine in all. The other three were "pay-on-arrival" guys. We slipped sixteen hundred dinar into our car-registration papers when the guard checked them. To give you an idea, a Coke costs about one dinar. And we got through. The guard just told us off a bit. He thought we were completely hilarious. We also gave him coffee and hashish. "You never saw me." Everyone says that the whole time. "You never saw me."

'In Tripoli we stayed in Souq al Jum'aa, the Friday-market district. I didn't have to contribute anything for rent or food; it was the end of the month and also I was the youngest. I went to look for my cousin Moussa at the hostel where the Zarma guys were staying. Like me, he was from the Poudrière neighbourhood of Niamey. But they told me: "Moussa has gone home." Their description of him was accurate. I was disheartened. I did see a guy called Moussa, also from Poudrière, but not my cousin Moussa.

'So we went under the freeway bridges to find work. An Arab can take you on to clean his house for twenty or thirty dinars. We communicated via hand gestures. But after a week, still no work. We were surprised to see Arabs working. "Those beautiful white-skinned people, working?" That was no good, that meant there was no work for us. In fact, they turned out to be Egyptians. We were relieved.

'Finally, I got a job carrying sand on a site where a house was being built. Thirty dinars. At last I was earning something. I also did *malga*, a bit of a painting. I learned my first words of Arabic. I went to the Nigerien embassy to ask for a job as a driver. The embassy was still open, but they didn't take me, even though they knew my uncle. We stayed in unfinished houses. It was very hot. It was summer. In one of the houses a bunch of robbers tricked me about some work and jumped me. The Moussa guy who wasn't the other Moussa paid them for me. But they broke my arm. It was shit. I went looking for some friends. I told them I was from Poudrière, they took me to hospital. The doctors wanted to know if I had been drinking alcohol. They made the gesture of drinking. No, no. The man who looked after the plaster casts kept saying *ghadaan*, tomorrow. A white nurse, a Filipino woman, begged the doctor by taking his two hands and saying, a plaster only takes five minutes. The prescriptions were going to cost eighty-five dinars and I only had five. I also had a bump on my head. I didn't want to go to sleep; the nurse had told me definitely not to sleep given my situation. My mate Moussa from Poudrière lent me ten dinars and we bought some Tramadol and antibiotics for fifteen dinars.

'After ten days I took off my plaster so I could work. This arm is still no good. It's the weakness in this arm that made me fall off the truck in Calais. Then at the *baldiyah*, at the town hall, I found some work, I emptied rubbish bins, sometimes I took clothes out of them for myself. I had terrible migraines. I took Efferalgan but it only worked for an hour. I stayed lying down. I stopped eating. August and September passed. I was alone. The Nigerien ambassador got me some Nifluril. In October I was able to go back to the town hall. I got a job as caretaker in an Italian man's house. I was earning two hundred dollars a month. I met Harbi, an Algerian, who was doing the electrical wiring in the house. He kept saying to me, "You must not steal, you must not lie, you can't trust anyone." Then I was a caretaker for an Iraqi. I got to eat well at his place. Then I found work at Misrata, where there was that massacre of the black population. I was doing pencil drawings. In forty days I earned a thousand dinars, it was good. Then I found a job at Al-Khums, which used to be a seaside resort. I did house painting for the local clan. There were a thousand unfinished houses, built for the English, for the oil-exploration industry. The clan had taken over all of them, although they didn't manage to live in them all.

'Then I was in Sirte, Gaddafi's last bastion. Then I was in Bani Walid, where there is one large tribe. They're the ones who broke my teeth. I couldn't get out of Libya. I think I was trapped by some mystical power. Libya was like being stuck in glue. I dreamed about an aeroplane, about taking off, being a bird. We were in the blazing sun behind wire fences and they burned us with irons to make us pay. Even children, even little kids. The screaming was the worst. A man came and paid for me and told me I'd be leaving from Tripoli. He said his name was Moussa, another

Moussa. I left with him, in the boot of his car. All I can remember is that we went very fast, because I had a really bad headache again. This Moussa also kept saying, "You never saw me." I ended up believing it. Did I see all that? He took the last of my money. And he robbed my mother: he made me give him her phone number. I had reached rock bottom. It was night on the beach in Tripoli and there were a whole lot of us. All of us black. People crouched round a few small fires. It was cold. I thought: this is antiquity. As for the sea, even though you might know how to swim, the amount of time a tree stays in water will never turn it into a crocodile. When I saw your ship, I thought I had died. It was so huge and bright, it looked like a rocket ship. I thought: either this is death, or else it's science fiction.'

She has written it all down, but he wants to go to London, to run into the future along roads where you are not asked for your identity papers. So Rose keeps working. The patients flock to her. She doesn't cure cancers, but she douses a few flames of anxiety and even takes some of the heat out of chemotherapy cases. In a single session, she relieves Delphine of her sciatica. She revitalises the fatigued. She refocuses people who are feeling bleary. She also provides mainstream courses of treatment. She adapts her prices: the rich pay for the poor. Regardless, her salary has skyrocketed from what it was in Paris. At the rate of ten or so sessions a day, even after the utility costs, couldn't they get a real concrete in-ground swimming pool? In between patients, she gets quotes online. Couldn't she pay for his damn border crossing to England? In the meantime, she makes a donation of three hundred, no, two hundred and fifty euros to the Catholic Relief Services—sixty-six per cent tax-deductible.

Arnaud has understood that his attempts to go into business with her are in vain. One-on-one is her thing. A pure and simple transfer. She doesn't take groups and stays clear of group trances. She has settled for trying to relieve suffering. He claims she's frightened of ghosts. He has a disapproving attitude to her consulting room and cites a feng-shui text to her: 'If the patient–doctor area is too spread out, the feminine energy tends to disappear and the women become dominant, in contradiction to their nature and to the detriment of everyone's health.'

In the village people are badmouthing her. Nathalie the physio will no longer talk to her.

Sometimes she misses the anonymity of Paris. She had seen Clèves as a refuge. But the huge upheaval in the world rattles her even here. In between patients, when no one is watching her, she makes the water in her glass wobble with the sheer power of her mind.

Meanwhile, Younès is bike-riding and it's doing wonders for his ankles. Rose runs behind, pushing the seat and *whoosh*, off he goes. He is very tall and Gabriel's bike is small, so he ends up in a diamond shape of arms and skinny legs.

'Yee-haw! Jiminy Cricket!' It's Raphaël Bidegarray jogging home from the fruit-and-vegetable depot. She never returned his call. Would he have a clue how to ride a dromedary? And all the sporty people from the village have a go at yelling out encouragements, like at the circus. But Younès is not a child; he is simply a Nigerien on a bike. She runs after him in a way that she never ran after her son when they took off his training wheels.

The river is sparkling, three swallows appear as black spots in her eyes, and the bike zigzags ahead, faster and faster. She stops, concentrates, her fists clenched, as tense as a pole vaulter, her eyes shut, standing poised, upright, slipping into a narrow passage, and when she opens her eyes again, a perfectly happy Younès is riding the bike like a champion.

Gabriel takes the school bus at six-thirty every morning. At six-thirty in the evening, when he arrives home, he finds Younès and his little sister in front of the cartoons on the TV. And when he comes home early on Wednesdays, at one o'clock, Younès is not up yet. Or he's playing on the Wii, Gabriel's Wii, with Emma. Gabriel locks himself in his beautiful feng shui room. Is he sulking? Is he bored? Is he filled with fury or gloom?

Rose promises them that Younès will leave. He doesn't want them to send him to school when the new school year starts. He doesn't want a part-time job in the library, even though they'd take him without identity papers. He doesn't want anything, not even asylum. So he'll leave, for sure.

Rose invites her son to lunch in South B, just the two of them. In the car, they both stare at the road. Through her laying on of hands, she'd like to smooth the wrinkles on his young forehead. She promises him that he can go to Paris for university, they'll work it out, he won't have to put up with the provincial clowns any longer. 'No one says clowns anymore, Mum, even in the provinces.' They smile at each other.

They sit out on the terrace of the restaurant, the sea is beautiful, it's May, the first tourists are eating ice-creams at Glaces Lopez. The novel Gabriel is writing is right there, in his phone. But it's a long way off being finished. 'You're writing a novel?' Gabriel looks out at the sea. We know what it's like with adolescents: they tell you a tiny bit of all the big things they have in their hearts. Rose wants to kiss him, her son, her marvellous son. She settles for touching his cheek with the end of her finger, and what takes place is precisely that: a caress.

Rose calls Solange on Skype: Gabriel is writing a novel. With all the contacts Solange has, surely she can find him a publisher, a producer, a scriptwriter, whatever, especially since she even knows George Clooney. But Solange wants to talk about Younès: his ankles, his past, his present, his future. She's been seized by a passion for Younès. She is going to send him some money.

Rose objects. 'It'll end up in the pocket of a people-smuggler.'

'But, of course, this young man must *cross the*

border,' Solange shoots back. 'We're not going to let him fall apart all over again.'

The 'we' annoys Rose, as much as the casual use of the words 'cross the border'. Solange, with everything she has, always feels the need to take from Rose the little she has. It's the evening in Beverly Hills, and Rose's house in Clèves, so pretty, so feng shui, seems pathetic compared with the enormous window looking out over the palm trees. Solange has a way of seeing her own reflection everywhere, so she identifies with Younès, even daring to compare herself with him: she too left when she was very young, with nothing but her hands in her pockets. Rose is fed up with Solange's saga. Because what was actually in her pockets, hey? There was a passport, certainly a tourist visa that allowed her to hole up in America well over the legal time limit. And it was a French passport, not a Nigerien passport. And her white woman's skin: shall we talk about her white woman's skin?

What Solange cannot take from her is what Rose has in her hands. She prefers to keep to herself how much her power seems to have grown stronger, here—matured, ripened like the mangoes beneath the desert rains.

Okay, fine about the money. Solange has already

helped her out several times. Younès doesn't have a bank account, but, yes, he has a phone number. Reluctantly, she gives her the number. Yes, it's the same number Gabriel has. That Gabriel had before. Yes. Now she has to tell her what happened. The cruise.

'Oh, that's right, you went on a cruise.' Solange gives the same light-hearted laugh she gave when Rose first mentioned the cruise to her; affectionate, of course, but so extraordinarily condescending that Rose could howl with rage. That condescension is like a bite, an electric charge—a Taser.

'You stole your son's phone to give it to Younès?' Now Solange is hiccupping with laughter, over there under the palm trees, her little svelte body flickering under the lights of the cinematographic night.

'I needed mine for *professional* reasons,' snarls Rose.

Behind the screen of Skype and of Hollywood, Solange taps her own phone: 'Two thousand dollars— which should appear in your account tomorrow, my dear. Give it to Younès and tell him it's from me.' Rose doesn't dare say that it's not enough.

She goes sales shopping with Emma in North B, a

girls' day. Emma's epidermis can no longer tolerate anything but untreated organic cotton; it's tricky to find, but there's no point in getting annoyed, she'll pay whatever it costs.

This little girl is a daydreamer, smart, a bit of a witch, and that augurs well for a future that may turn out to be more magical than envisaged. For her birthday she wants an iPhone, a real one, like everyone, even Younès has one. With a unicorn case. Right now, she wants to eat McDonald's. At least it won't be expensive. Rose gets a salad and a cut-up apple while Emma does battle with a Big Mac. It's not going to be good for her eczema, but the view is so pretty. Is there any other McDonald's in the world with such a beautiful view over the sea? They eat lunch on the terrace and the Adour River pours into the Atlantic. The river is zinc-grey over the milky blue of the sea, a two-tone, liquid landscape, fresh water flowing into salty water.

Emma laughs at the sparrows that have come to pinch the crumbs.

'Do you remember, darling, in Paris, how the sparrows were disappearing?'

Those ordinary little brown birds, a bird so perfect we believed it would be there forever, *cheep*

cheep, and the breadcrumbs, flocks of sparrows under the chairs on the terraces. Emma chirps as she pecks at her burger. She knows nothing about extinction or disappearance, despite her own disappearance at the Parthenon. She's telling Rose how she can zypnotise the birdz. And in five minutes time she'll be writhing in pain with indigestion. Illogicality, lack of foresight, fantasising: the three treasures of childhood.

On the way home, Rose leaves her nauseated child in the car while she runs in quickly to enrol in the most popular Pilates class on the coast. It's a forty-five-minute drive from Clèves, but it's worth it. She gets out her credit card and has a moment of disbelief: she thought it was twenty euros per class, but it's twenty euros per *month*. She pays up immediately. She'll come once a week. Getting out of breath running after Younès on the bike has made her realise she's not getting any younger.

She can't say the patients are tiring her out; it's not like in the handbook of magic that Arnaud lent her: she's not feeling drained from giving out her fluid, no. But her muscles are getting stiffer and stiffer. When she was a psychologist pure and simple, apart from the more physical sessions, like those with Bilal, she remained seated, dreamy, in that state of floating attentiveness that conjures up an evening by the fire: the patient's words crackle, sentences are tinged with bluish glimmers, time smoulders…but if a log falls, or a word pops, if a sentence ignites in a burst of brightness, you are there. Occasionally you have to leap up from your chair. Sometimes you blow on the coals. But here, in Clèves, she has accepted to be right in the fire. She leans over the bodies, and those bodies speak, or don't speak.

Arnaud can't stand his clients chattering. He stuck a red drawing pin in the ceiling, and he asks them to concentrate on it in silence while he *does his thing*. Groups of people have to stare at the drawing pin too. The Sacred Pin. Rose is sceptical. Anyone can criticise Freud these days, but we let unauthorised practitioners run wild. And, as far as clinical effectiveness goes, Arnaud seems so tortured that Rose wonders if he isn't in fact propagating the demons himself.

She waits for Younès to finish praying on the rug at the end of the couch. It's safe to say that they are not taking any chances. Then she lies him down. She gently places her fingers on his temples. His blood is pounding. She murmurs the preliminary phrases to him: your body is heavy. Heavy from your head to your feet. Your joints are heavy, all your limbs are heavy. Younès's modesty is extreme, so Rose goes into no further detail, merely alluding to his body as a thin and strong entity that will get across the border. She summons up the water that flows, the wind that blows, the sea that swells and retreats, sap that rises in plants and time without constraints: whatever comes and goes, everything that runs. It takes hold of her like a song. It's the crossing-the-border song. Her crooning French mingles with the echoes of the prayer in Zarma that hangs in the room. Half-drawn curtains, half-closed eyes; they are on the edge of sleep, drifting off at the edge of the sea.

'Younès,' says Rose softly.

'*Ay gono*,' says Younès.

She moves her hands above his belly. Modesty itself becomes like a fluid between them. The heat circulates: thighs, knees, ankles, feet, hands, head, heart, everything he will need in order to brave the border. Let's treat it as a preparation, training. She sees the border crossing as two blades of time moving apart. She sees two sheets of air; she is at their confluence. She remembers herself as a child in the fern-covered mountain above Clèves, one foot in Spain and the other in France, trying to *feel* the border, its disturbing unreality. She was a child who was amazed by the invisible. And through Younès's bones she can feel his childhood; she can feel his strength, his fragility, and the violation of his failure to anticipate the future, everything that Younès has had to learn so fast inside death's wet grasp.

She lets the images run. She does not stop a single one. A dark shape approaches her. Is it one of those beings that can walk through walls, those elusive creatures that no house can contain? She saw engravings of them in Arnaud's handbook of magic. She would like to modify the substance that constitutes Younès, equip him with the DNA of a cat, an eel, a lizard, a swallow. She would like to give him the attributes of animals who can slip, slither, slide; cover his bones with a metamorphic body; graft wings onto him and a long skin that weaves and wends. The room is full of waves of energy, whisperings, scratching, little shrieks. The curtain flutters and settles, the house heaves a sigh, the walls disintegrate. The air looks like water and the water looks like sand. Rose and Younès are two birds, two fish, soon two snakes.

'Now,' says Rose. The word stays there, doesn't take off. She catches hold of Younès's hands, slides his arms onto her shoulders. *Hup.* She lifts him up, with every bit of strength in her legs and her belly. He goes along with the movement. He grows lighter. He surrenders and helps her. She carries him. She carries him on her back. She lifts him off the floor. There's a sound: *click*. The two of them start to float.

They have a coffee after the session. Lots of sugar for him, as always, with sweet biscuits. If Younès now has wings, or a body made of some modified substance, it's not visible. And Rose is not tired; she feels great. She talks to him about Gabriel, about his plans to study in Paris, about the novels he's writing.

'He writes because he's in a safe place,' says Younès sententiously.

'He writes because he has talent,' Rose protests.

Younès hisses through his saliva. 'I eat, therefore I write.'

'Oh, you're so annoying,' says Rose, as she clears away the cups and biscuits.

She drives to her Pilates class. The room in the warehouse near the airport is gigantic. It's eleven o'clock, the plane from Paris is turning towards the sea. The din of the jet engines. The class is working on what in Paris they call downward dog; here it's simply the dog. Then they come back up, vertebra by vertebra, each person in their own rhythm: exhale as you rise and gently open your arms, imagine your head suspended by a thread attached to the ceiling, keep your hands in your field of vision and stretch from the hook of your bra top, below the shoulder blades for the guys, careful, I do not want anyone holding their breath. It's the same routine as in Paris but with a different accent. In front of her, lots of backsides rise, lots of vertebrae beneath assorted T-shirts, rugby or the brand 64 or Quiksilver or Pétrole Hahn *for strong, healthy hair* or Atlantic Multiservices, *Lassaga father and son house painting.*

She always arrives at the school slightly late, the traffic jams are a good excuse, when the truth is she would rather not have to chat with Lætitia, still as chic and thin as ever, a flat belly and four children with Basque names (Gorka, Haize, Itsas and Oihan: the less you are from around here, the more inclined you are to do things the Basque way); she'd rather avoid the principal of the school, because really, what can she do, they move eight hundred kilometres, they change their meteorological and social climate, everything, so that Emma can come out of class minus a lock of hair chopped off with scissors, by Itsas, to be exact, a seven-year-old girl, leader of a band of little bitches who make fun of Emma's accent, but even so, they're not going to send her to the Montessori, or to the nuns thirty kays away. In Niamey, she'd have a tray on her head and sell individual cigarettes in the street, end of story.

But that's not it, it's not her accent, it's not that she's new. 'It's, how shall we say, that strangeness that belongs to her'—the principal takes a step back because the eyes of our dear psychologist are blazing—'it's just that your daughter frightens the other children a little bit.' They're saying that she zypnotises them. Apparently, parents are complaining that their kids are coming down with strange aches and pains. Unbelievable.

Only Younès manages to distract Emma. They play Monopoly for hours: seven years old and twenty kilos of itching, twenty years old and sixty kilos of yearning to leave, swapping rue de la Paix for a hotel on rue de Vaugirard, things are not really looking great in their lives for either of them.

Come on. Breathe. Your lower back is drawing in your navel, your nape is supple. The sun pours in through an odour of kerosene. The weather is lovely.

At 11.20 a.m. it's the plane from Stockholm, which only flies from May to September. At midday it's the plane for Madrid. A bit later there'll be the one from Lyon, and around it goes like a little clock, four or five destinations out of this spot at the bottom of the Bay of Biscay. And when you think about Orly airport, or Roissy…Admittedly, she never flies. But still. It's the principle of it. The *possibility* of leaving. She feels slightly claustrophobic as she heads back to her village, careful, no holding your breath.

He sits down cross-legged on the rug, as he likes to do now that he has recovered the flexibility in his ankles. She is in her armchair, clicking around the internet. They go through their plan again. Clèves–Calais: North B station then change at Paris-Nord for Calais-Ville, stay clear of cops, tickets in order, paid for by Rose, head straight for the Total petrol station, avoid people-smugglers.

She made him promise not to take the Eurostar: It's not the right expression, to not *try to cross* via the Eurostar.

'You talk like my mother,' says Younès, smiling. 'For her it was the boat, for you the train. The metal gates are too high, it's too *riskful* now, no one even jumps off the bridges onto the trucks anymore.'

He's talking about Calais like a seasoned strategist, as if he had investigated a manoeuvre, paced it out, penetrated the area, evaluated it from the perspective of its flaws, a country to get out of.

'The tunnel,' says Younès, 'is the mouth of the wolf. You've seen *Star Wars*? There's a beast in the dune, an enormous worm. You can only see its mouth. A big hole full of teeth that opens in the sand. That's what the tunnel reminds me of. Also in *Star Wars*, there's a bar in space, with space monsters. There's the Jedi, he's looking for a bad guy, and there's a boy selling drugs. The boy is like a mosquito, he keeps coming back all the time with his bad attitude and he stops the Jedi from finding the bad guy. Well, he's not really *stopping* him because nothing stops the Jedi, who is as powerful as Saladin, but there's the boy, like a fly, so the Jedi passes his hand in front of the boy's eyes, without even looking at him, just like that, he passes his hand in front of his eyes and says to him, "You must change your life."'

'That's a line from Rilke,' says Rose, moved. She studied German as her first foreign language, not Spanish like the rest of the village. Her parents thought it would be better for finding her direction, not in space, but in her social class.

'It's a line from the Jedi,' Younès insists. 'Those words have stayed with me.' And he repeats them, his hands on his knees, as if he's praying. *You must change your life.*

Ten years later, Rose waits under Brixton Bridge. She is still married to her husband. Gabriel is dragging out a PhD in literature that is costing them a fortune, but he's finished a first novel, so we'll see. Emma is studying for her baccalaureate with the nuns in West C and she continues to suffer from allergies that pose questions about the future liveability of this planet.

It is the world that should have changed, not your life. That's what Rose is thinking as she waits for Younès to meet her under Brixton Bridge in London. Brixton Bridge in London—she has plenty of time to study it—is a viaduct above the Brixton tube station. Plants, rust and graffiti have made a meal of it, but you can imagine it still standing in a post-human city: a disproportionately large overpass for whatever insects and crawling creatures are left, beneath a sun heading to the end of its future as a star, burning the last of its hydrogen, then, at the end of the thousands of years that were once human, devouring its final reserves of helium, in a wild expenditure of energy, a space junkie's fireworks, an intergalactic last stand, for no reason, no one there, gobbling everything, swallowing up Mercury, Venus and the Earth, rolling out unimaginable flames, whirling in its own star-junk, spinning its own destruction in revolutions, a red giant then a white dwarf, its core collapsing in on itself, discharging the last of its matter in a multicoloured carnival unseen by any eye from ancient Earth.

It's the first time Rose has been to London. She took the Eurostar. A celebration. She travelled through the tunnel, that marvel of human ingenuity. Her passport was in order at the check-in. She took the tube, and now Rose Goyenetche is waiting for Younès Aboussa under the Brixton Bridge with a certain degree of anxiety, because if he doesn't show up she'll have to work out how to spend a day in London; it reminds her of that memorable day in Calais. But then again, it's London; perhaps she'll go to the British Museum. She doesn't want to. She wants to see him.

There he is. She recognises him immediately in the crowd of black people in Brixton. He gives her a wave. Her anxiety disappears. He has bulked up; he wears his braided hair close to his skull and a hiphop-style vest that shows off his muscled shoulders. He holds out his hand, she touches it and there's a little *zap* that makes them laugh, and he gives her a big hug and lifts her up and they twirl around under the Brixton Bridge.

'Now,' Younès had said ten years earlier, or rather he wrote it in a text, *ping*, but just in case, she had already been sending all her energy towards the north for over an hour. Just in case, she had also given him four thousand euros in cash (Solange's two thousand, plus two thousand from her work sessions: he wouldn't hear of her giving him more, and honestly, *phew*). In the Calais region, over the summer solstice, the sun sets an hour later than in the Basque Country, due to the Earth's tilt. In winter it's the opposite, it sets earlier. Like two astronomers, they had discussed every step of the way and worked out a timetable so that she could send her waves of energy at the right moment. She had never attempted to engage in this remotely, or only very occasionally, out of superstition: a prayer for her husband when he went off to make a diffi-cult sale, and sometimes for Bilal, and telepathically for Grichka, but it was only for a second, hey, almost without thinking; everyone does that, don't they? Or for those kids stuck in a cave in Thailand a long time ago, or even longer ago, for those miners stranded underground in Mexico, and it seemed to her as if that had worked, that it was harmless—her own sort of prayer for those who were caught in a trap.

'Now,' says Younès's text, and she sends him everything she is capable of. It's concentrated, it comes out of her through her whole head and through the centre of her chest, the two fluids mingling in a hot red whirlwind. She's Wonder Woman: her hands start up, it's coming out of her hands too, her hands, her best allies—she holds them out in front of her. For a long time, human beings wrote with only one hand; now they type with two on their keyboards, which has undermined the laterality of *Homo sapiens* and the balance of the brain's hemispheres—she has theories about all this. She is frightened for him. In the end, the creature who walks through walls gets stuck in the wall. What sort of a life would he have in the wall?

To make sure she wouldn't be disturbed, she told everyone that she was on a Skype consultation in her office. And it's a bit like Skype except the screen is in her head, Younès's image is bouncing about as if they were on Skype and the message is going in one direction; if it was spoken out loud it would be nothing more than 'go for it' or 'cross'. This is it. It's now. She feels an enormous sense of release. The molecules of the obstacle separate into atoms that are pulverised into neutrons that dissolve into nameless states of matter. Through. It's turning into dust. It's dispersing. It's global. The border has given way.

Unusual psychologist that she is, she falls asleep abruptly in her armchair, and stays there. It's only the quality of her consciousness that has altered. Yes, Rose Goyenetche is with us. She sees Younès in front of a huge wall that has become fluid; he is swimming inside the wall, atomised, moving forward easily through its entire thickness; he looks happy. The wall dissolves again and becomes gaseous, a cloud, air. Younès swims, he flies, Grichka has entrusted him with his helmet, and there is Gabriel hunched over his phone, and there is Emma, super-powerful and healed, and Veronika L., resolutely alive and chatting with the relaxed tenant, and her husband, sober and cheerful. Everyone is there and Younès is playing conductor of the orchestra—it's funny—with arm movements that unleash a phenomenal hot, dry Harmattan wind, the sky saturated with a whirlwind of red, orange and ochre particles. They have to shut their eyes and their mouths and cover their heads with their hands, bury themselves in their arms: well, anyway, it's a dream.

Her husband defies the prohibition and knocks on the door.

'Come in.' Rose rouses herself. She calls Younès, he doesn't answer, but it's ringing in England: the ringtone is English, *beep beep* instead of the French *dring dring*. She puts it on loudspeaker and laughs, and her husband takes her in his arms. Younès has crossed the border, he is out of the belly of the whale, he has been spat out again on the side of the shore he longed for.

They are in their big bed. They are safe. Life will go on. The wind from the south is leaning lightly on the house. Rose has fallen back to sleep next to her man. And in the morning, the terrace, facing the Pyrenees, is covered with a red veil of Sahara sand.

With thanks to:

Abdoul Aziz Albadja

Jean-Pierre Ariol

Mauro Armanino

Rita Bandinelli

Rolande Berger

Philippe Brachet

Sandrine Deloche

Martine Devries

Yann Diener

Hasier Etxeberria

Alexandra Galitzine-Loumpet

Anne Florence Garnier

Marc-André Gutscher

Patricia Fiske

Charles Freger

Jessica Jouve

Guillaume Langeon

Nathalie Lelong

Erica Mbiapep Wandjeh

Justyna Mielnikiewicz

Ibrahim Ngouwouo

Idi Nouhou

Alexis Nuselovici

Hania Osta

Philippe Quintin

Merveille Sangalé Guidjelie

Emmanuelle Touati

Benedict Wleh

Tom-Tom, Sylvie, Sylvain, Mariam, Nasrine, Jacob and David, Thomas and Thomas

A novel of cinema and desire.

WINNER, PRIX MÉDICIS & PRIX DES PRIX

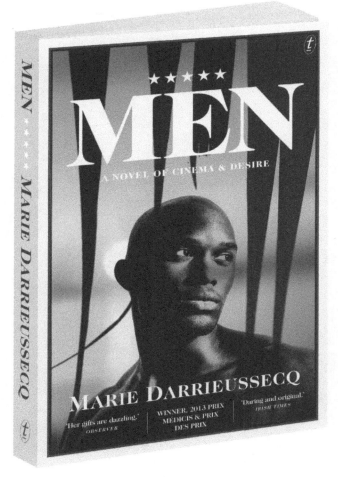

With her characteristic intensity, edginess
and humour, Marie Darriuessecq explores
female desire, what it means to be a woman.

TEXTPUBLISHING.COM.AU

Whatever it takes,
Solange will go all the way.

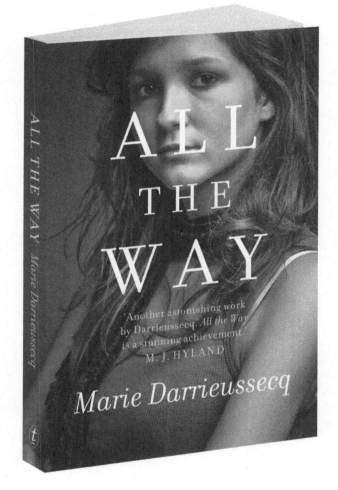

Brilliant and hilarious, *All the Way* offers an extraordinary
insight into the language and obsessions of adolescence,
by one of France's greatest living writers.

TEXTPUBLISHING.COM.AU

Artist and mother: the first woman
to paint herself naked, and pregnant.

A unique biography of the ground-breaking Expressionist
painter Paula Modersohn-Becker: her fraught marriage
and career, and her untimely death.

TEXTPUBLISHING.COM.AU

A fascinating tale that recalls
Darrieussecq's bestselling debut, *Pig Tales*.

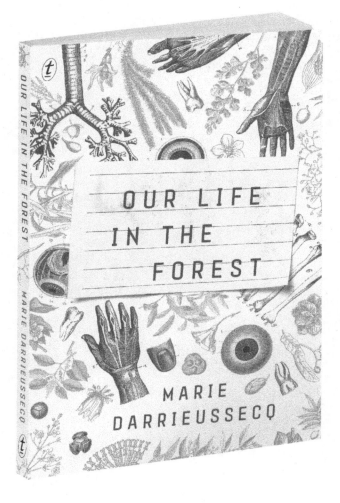

In the near future, a woman is writing in the forest. She has
fled the city, along with other fugitives and their 'halves'.
But the reanimated halves are behaving strangely…

TEXTPUBLISHING.COM.AU

I stopped despairing when a crèche materialised.

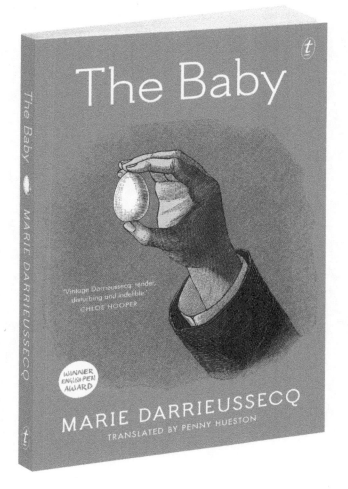

A mother's project and a writer's project—how to reconcile these two demanding roles? What is a baby? And why are there so few of them in literature?

TEXTPUBLISHING.COM.AU